Christopher Tull was born in 1936, the son of a country rector. Ordained in 1962, he spent all his ministry in parishes between Tiverton and South Molton in rural Devon. Now retired, he still lives in the West Country, devotes much of his time to writing, and remains active in church life.

GREENER GROWS THE GRASS

Christopher Tull

Broad Street Publishing

Printed and bound in Great Britain by
Short Run Press Limited, Exeter

BROAD STREET PUBLISHING
Arden Cottage, Coombeshead Road, Highweek,
Newton Abbot TQ12 1PZ
Tel +44 (0)1626 365478

For
The people of The Exe Valley and
Oakmoor Groups of Churches in Devon
amongst whom I spent many happy years of ministry

I would also like to express deep appreciation to Jiff Villiers for
kindly allowing me to reproduce watercolours from her book
To Stand and Stare – A Limited Edition of 200
Broad Street Publishing
ISBN 9780955701924

To Norman Dallyn who helped me with my word processing

To Chrissie and Mark Young of Broad Street Publishing
for their help and dedication to publishing my book

And last, but not least, to my wife Rosemary, who checked my
work and came up with good ideas when I got stuck.

From Christopher Tull's first book
In Pastures Green?

In 1957 Jack Longfield becomes rector of Ashenridge and Combe Peter, two sleepy rural parishes in the West Country. He and his wife, Mary, along with their two children, Paul and Ann, gradually settle in at the rectory. But Jack soon discovers that most of his parishioners want things to stay just the way they are and resent any kind of interference.

When the two nearby parishes of Westaleigh and Brookworthy come under his care, Jack's family life begins to suffer, but with the arrival of a new curate things can only get better, can't they?

Memorable characters leap off every page in this collection of warm-hearted tales about life in a rural parish. Many of them reappear in the book you are about to read.

Contents

Chapter 1

Blizzards and Blows

If only I'd looked in my diary. I still cringe when I think about it now. It was entirely my own silly fault.

Our sixth Christmas at Ashenridge had been one of the happiest ever. Mary's flamboyant cousin, Will, arrived on Christmas Eve, his first Christmas with us at the rectory. Mary constantly worried about his love of the bottle and there was no doubt he'd had a few by the time he got to us. Our children, thirteen-year-old Paul, and Ann, a year younger, loved Uncle Tiddly, a nickname they'd given him many years ago, and with good reason. Yet over Christmas he behaved impeccably and hardly touched a drop. Not for the first time Mary and I wondered if he was about to become a reformed character.

We sat round the fire on Christmas Day listening to Will's fascinating stories about his so-called acting career. We hardly watched the television, though Mary insisted we switch on at three o'clock to listen to the Queen's Speech. Will had an endless supply of jokes, and before each one he'd ask, 'Have you heard the one about...?' More often than not we had, but he still kept us in stitches.

On Boxing Day he surprised us all by announcing, "Had a splendid Christmas. You've done me proud. But you know what William says, 'time stands still for no man', so I'm off to London first thing in the morning." This was so typical of Will. Over the years we'd come to accept that he was always short of funds, always hatching plans that would make him a fortune. We simply assumed he'd come up with yet another brainwave.

As he pulled out of the drive I realised the rectory would seem quite empty without him, but then my thoughts turned to spending a few days alone with Mary and the children. I couldn't think of a better way to round off the year.

Saturday the 29th December 1962 is a day those living in the West Country will never forget. It had already been a very cold winter. Even in late November heavy snowfalls meant sheep on some upland farms had to be dug out of drifts. The snow returned on Boxing Day. At first it fell in light flurries, but come Saturday the sky was leaden and the wind bitterly cold. The lunchtime weather forecast warned of severe snowfalls and drifting. It was time to batten down the hatches.

"Jack, you really are being irresponsible," Mary insisted. "Wanting to drive twenty miles to Whiteminster on a day like this. We'll never get back."

"Yes, dear, I know how you feel," I replied, fiddling with the uncomfortable clerical collar I'd not worn since Christmas Day. "But I never managed to fit in some of my hospital visits, and they're just as important as the Christmas services."

"But Jack, we promised to take the children to friends on the outskirts of Leighford. Can't we leave it at that? Three miles is quite enough in these conditions."

"It would be if all our sick parishioners were in the cottage hospital."

"But can't you see? It's a crazy idea."

"Now listen, Mary. Whiteminster is on a main road. It's bound to stay open, so there's no need to panic. If we don't go today it could be weeks before we get there."

"All right," she agreed reluctantly. "But if we really must go it's essential we take boots, a shovel and sacking with us."

After lunch we dropped the children at their friends' house and drove on to the cathedral city. The journey took us along the deeply wooded Badger Valley, beautiful at any time of the year, magical now with its light covering of snow.

Mary kept glancing at the menacing sky. We agreed it would be wise to make our visit a short one, and while I paid my hospital visits Mary stocked up with extra food and essentials. From time to time I looked out of the hospital window. It was only three o'clock – it looked more like the middle of the night.

By the time we got to the outskirts of Leighford to collect Paul and Ann the east wind had picked up and the snow was blowing horizontally. Even during our brief stay at the house a drift had formed on the road outside. There was only one thing for it. I accelerated and drove straight at it, which brought screams of delight from the back of the car. As the road turned eastwards the snow no longer drifted across the road but blew straight at us. The windscreen wipers could barely cope. I was relieved to find the traffic still running freely when we reached the centre of Leighford, but that was the easy bit. We now faced a three-mile climb up a narrow road to our home in Ashenridge.

The first part of the journey was not too bad because the road was sheltered by a high hedge. However, as we gained height and the hedge lowered, the wind drove the snow with all its might against the left bank of the lane. I could see wheel tracks ahead and prayed the vehicle in front didn't get stuck because that would finish us. We reached the top and the tracks we were following disappeared. In desperation I accelerated and drove with all my might into the blinding storm. As we slithered round I could feel the snow hard against the axles. It would only be a matter of minutes before we got completely stuck. Then I felt the tyres grip and we were off again. Mercifully, the tracks we had been following reappeared.

"Dad, how long do you think we could survive if we got stuck in a drift?" Ann sounded excited.

Paul chipped in. "I once read about a family who got buried in a snow drift and were pulled out alive after three days."

"And do you remember that scary story Uncle Tiddly told us about a man being frozen? He was turned into a block of ice, just like the Bible story where Lot's wife was turned into a pillar of salt. Anyway, when the snow covered him he looked just like a snowman. Uncle Tiddly said that's how the word snowman got its name, and..."

"That's enough." Mary's voice was shaking and her hands were clasped tightly in her lap.

To my horror I now saw rear lights ahead. The last thing we needed was to meet another car, but then I realised it was a stationary Land Rover. Assuming it was stuck I pulled up and frantically blew the horn.

To my amazement, a figure appeared and signalled for us to follow. Off he drove, charging through drifts and blowing back so much snow I could barely follow his lights. After what seemed an age we reached Ashenridge and I honked several times to thank our unknown guide. The drive leading to the rectory was deep in snow, but nothing compared to the hills we'd just climbed. We quickly unloaded the car, slammed the front door shut, and prepared for the worst.

My curate, Roy Edwards, and his wife, Lucy, had been spending a couple of days after Christmas with her mother in the Home Counties. The snow started falling there before it really got going further west and they decided to leave their car behind and come back by train. It stopped at every little junction and they wondered if they would ever get home.

When they arrived at Whiteminster Station the little push and pull train for Leighford was waiting in the platform bay. Roy had the good sense to ring a friend who said he would meet them off the train. By now it was pitch black and the heavy snow was turning into a full-scale blizzard.

Thanks to a snow plough the line was still running, and in fact remained open all through that terrible winter, only to be closed the following autumn under the Beeching Axe.

Roy and Lucy were relieved to find their friend waiting for them at Leighford Station. It needed his Land Rover to negotiate the dreadful conditions, but even so they had a hair-raising journey and let out a cheer when Westaleigh Vicarage came into sight.

As the full force of the blizzard took hold, one of Ashenridge's church wardens, Colonel Waters, struggled to close his front door. 'Poor rector', he thought to himself. 'Wouldn't like to be in his shoes when the Hawkes family catch up with him'.

At the village shop Mr Radd was relieved his wholesaler had made a delivery that morning. During the afternoon several locals had popped in to stock up on essentials – and to ask if he happened to know the whereabouts of Mr Longfield? By four o'clock the whole village was deserted.

That evening snow drifts were enveloping the bus shelter in the centre of the village. On fine days, this is where Kitty would hold court with her little knot of elderly ladies. She now looked disapprovingly as her granddaughter, Becky, brought in yet more coal and wood. "'Tiddn' true what they'm sayin' on the wireless 'bout the weather. They'm makin' it up. You ask the rector what 'e thinks, that's if yer can find 'im!"

Mrs Batchelor's drawing room felt unusually chilly. She was particularly concerned about keeping the right temperature for her pots of pink lilies. They so hated the cold. She gazed fondly at them and wondered if the ones she'd put in the church for Christmas had survived. They would be just right for the Andrew Hawkes baptism.

Little Billy Hawkes knelt by his bed and prayed harder than he'd ever prayed before. "Please Jesus, please let it go on snowing and don't let it melt." Mrs Hawkes gave her son a fond look, put his smart blue suit back on its hanger and kissed him goodnight. Billy had been disappointed not to see his baby brother, Andrew, being baptised, but all the same he hoped the rector wouldn't want him to wear that awful suit again tomorrow. He'd much rather play in the snow.

Church services in all four parishes were out of the question that Sunday. I was anxious about Roy and Lucy and tried ringing them again…the line was still dead. I stood in my freezing cold study feeling totally disorientated. All normal activities had come to a halt and I began wondering who might need help or if any events needed cancelling. Glancing down at my diary an entry leapt out at me: Ashenridge Church – Sat 29th December – 3pm Baptism of Andrew Hawkes. My heart sank!

Back in September Tom Hawkes had pressed me into holding his son's baptism on a Saturday because it was the only day the whole family could be together. I normally held baptisms on Sunday afternoons – the newer custom of holding them during a service hadn't yet taken root in my parishes. He'd made it difficult for me to say 'no', and the 29th December was agreed.

The Hawkes family lived in a farmhouse on the other side of Brookworthy and were known to me more by reputation than anything else. Tom's father – one of the leading farmers in the district who owned four other farms – had died that spring. Unlike his father, Tom never flashed money around and his reputation for being mean spread when he wrote to his tenants increasing their rents.

He'd sat in my study all those months ago telling me how Ashenridge was the old family home, which was why he wanted the service there. I must confess I'd avoided telling Mary because I knew she'd be upset at having to give up yet another 'home day', our nickname for Saturdays.

Parishioners will usually forgive their clergy for making mistakes, and generally read their lapses in a good light, but to forget a baptism was unforgiveable. I tried the phone again. It was still dead, and at that moment I wished I was too.

Chapter 2

'Tiddn' All Bad

"The poor Hawkes family. I've let them down so badly. If only I had looked in my diary and remembered Andrew's baptism. If only..."

Mary put a hand on my shoulder. "Come on, Jack, we all make mistakes. I'm sure they'll understand."

It was no good. The blizzard had put paid to the telephone, and there was unlikely to be any post for days. I was powerless to do anything about my blunder. "It's not just the Hawkes family. What about their friends. What if some of them have been stranded?"

The wind roared down the study chimney sending flurries of snow into the hearth. Mary tried to distract me by asking about the lights. I went off to find candles, but still couldn't get the Hawkes family out of my mind. If only I could contact them, but to try and reach them in this weather would be like Oates leaving his tent at the South Pole.

The storm dragged on, we were running short of fuel, and Paul spent hours sawing up half-green wood which gave out little heat. There were days when the sun shone, but it was so cold the snow didn't melt. Some people attempted to clear the roads, but it was a thankless task. Farmers were busy tending their livestock; the engineers couldn't reach the telephone or electric cables, and to make matters worse the pumping machines for the mains water failed.

The rectory had a deep well under the scullery floor. Not long after our arrival the diocese had put us on mains water, removed the huge hand pump that drew water up to the tank in the roof, and sealed the whole thing over. Fortunately we had a retired plumber living in the village and he now made a small opening in the floor, inserted a long plastic tube and fixed a modern hand pump beside the scullery sink. The water came flowing through and before long people were coming to us for supplies. A couple of local lads were keen to help and attached a plastic drum to our sledge, delivering water to anyone who needed it. I was most impressed until I discovered they were charging for this service!

As we came to terms with what was happening everyone did their best to help one another. Mrs Mathilda Pink, a public-spirited war widow, was very concerned about the Hartons, an old couple living in a remote spot on Ashenridge Moor who for years had depended on others for their food. Mrs Pink's sports-mad niece, Angela, had been forced to extend her stay because of the bad weather, and when there was a brief respite at the beginning of January she came up with a brilliant idea. If her aunt would cook a couple of meals, she'd put them in a rucksack along with some bread and milk and ski over to Woods Cottage.

The Hartons were huddled together trying to get some warmth from a meagre fire when the knock came at their door.

It took a startled Mrs Harton several seconds to undo the heavy bolts. To her amazement before her stood the most beautiful girl she had ever seen, her long golden hair shining in the sunlight. Her skis, now tucked behind her, resembled wings. Her beautiful face radiated light and glory. Mrs Harton was convinced she had come face to face with an angel – an angel offering her a gift that smelt of turkey. She remembered distant Sunday School stories – huge black ravens feeding meat and bread to Elijah; the angel Gabriel appearing before Mary. Open-mouthed and speechless, she crossed herself, bowed, and held out her trembling hands to accept the gift. Angela asked if there was anything she could do to help, but Mrs Harton was already closing the door, too overcome to answer.

For months anyone visiting Woods Cottage would be treated to her incredible story. One day she asked me if I believed in angels. I told her I most certainly did – and I meant it.

As the days went by, everyone learnt to live with the severe weather. I still had no way of contacting the Hawkes family and remained deeply disturbed about it.

My good-natured sexton, Len Cooksley, told me how they'd waited in the cold church that Saturday. "Three times I went round to your rectory, but 'twas empty. Your name was mud, rector, but when they seed 'ow the weather was disintergratin' they all went 'ome. I told they there must've been a cata...a catastro..." Len paused and scratched his head. "I told they somethin' awful must've 'appened to keep rector from a baptism."

It was Len who told me that the Rendalls, an elderly couple at Withycombe Farm, were having trouble locating some of their sheep. Armed with shovels and long wooden rods, Paul and Ann joined me on a quest to find them. Mr Rendall was a bit vague about their whereabouts, but Paul spotted a ewe half-hidden in a drift in the next field. It was going to be difficult reaching her, but the snow against the hedge was firm so we clambered over and dropped several feet down on to the lee side. I guessed the other ewes must be close by and gently prodded with the rod. It passed through several feet of snow before touching something soft. We kept digging and found several of the sheep alive. I was surprised by the number. From what Mr Rendall had said I'd expected just a few, yet we counted twenty live and six dead.

By now the wind was picking up and I was concerned about the sheep we'd dug out. Most of them had managed to stumble towards a patch of grass where the wind had blown the snow clear, but they were dreadfully exposed to the harsh weather.

As we approached the farm I could see Mr Rendall in the yard, a shovel in one hand and some sorry-looking ewes close by. I called out to him in triumph about the sheep we'd found. Instead of looking pleased he shook his head in disbelief and said the ewes in that field were nothing to do with him.

I now realised we had probably done more harm than good and it would have been kinder to leave the ewes in the relative security of their snowy cave. I begged some bales of hay from Mr Rendall. He was a bit reluctant at first, but let me have half-a-dozen along with some cord and old sheets of corrugated iron. Using the sheets we were able to slide the bales along the route we'd made over the field. Paul and Ann looked exhausted and it was nightfall before we'd finished, but at least the ewes had food and reasonable shelter.

The following day I returned to the farm to check up on the ewes. When I got there a party of men were lending a hand in the yard. Not being needed I turned towards the field and was amazed to see a solitary figure struggling there. I asked the men if they knew who it was.

"Oh, that's Tom Hawkes," one of them sneered. "He's got money enough. Robs his tenants that one. He can manage without the likes of us."

I could see they had no intention of helping me or Tom, but I didn't hesitate. Here was my long-awaited opportunity to apologise for forgetting his son's baptism.

I'd been surprised to see Tom in the field and he was even more surprised to see me. "Is that you, rector? I never expected to find you here." Then pointing to some sheep he asked, "Is this your work?"

I nodded. Tom pulled a handkerchief from his pocket and dabbed at his eyes with it. The poor man was crying. "Rector, I'm at the end of my tether. I've got about fifty sheep somewhere in that drift. Prize closewools due to lamb in March. If I lose them bang goes my best flock. Old man Rendall won't let me near his farm, so what can I do?"

"Look, is that your tractor?" I'd spotted a tractor and link box on the other side of the field. Tom nodded.

"Why don't you try to work your way there and at least we can get some of your flock to safety. Only it does depend on the weather," I added, looking up at the menacing sky.

Tom staggered off and was nearing the final hedge when he disappeared from sight. It took me quite a time to reach him. The poor man had gone right into a thorn bush and lay wedged between the unfriendly branches. Fortunately his layers of clothing had taken most of the punishment from the cruel spikes, but his head and hands were bleeding badly. He told me his feet were stuck, but as far as he could tell nothing was broken. Remembering my wartime experiences in the Royal Army Medical Corps, I checked the little of him I could reach, left him reasonably comfortable and set off for help. By the time I got to the farm I was exhausted.

"Serves 'im right, the old bastard. Won't do 'im any 'arm to 'ave a taste of the cold."

I was taken aback by Mr Rendall's reaction, and it was only when I stressed the seriousness of the situation he agreed to help. We went as far as we could by tractor, Mr Rendall muttering all the time about messing up his hedges and how come next summer he'd have stock all over the place – *and* he'd be looking for compensation.

Carrying a makeshift stretcher and shovels, we got to Tom and freed him from his thorny tomb. It took a fair while to get back to the farm and Tom looked in a bad way.

While I removed his outer clothing Mrs Rendall filled hot-water bottles, and we spent the next hour or so thawing out and drinking endless cups of tea laced with whisky. Tom's colour slowly returned, and although it was probably the whisky talking, once he'd got started he couldn't stop.

"That was one of my father's best fields, and one the old man would never let out to any other tenant." Looking straight at Mr Rendall he continued. "I know you turned it down after dad died, and I can understand why, especially with the increased rent. The truth is my father lived in a fool's paradise, throwing money around while the whole business was going downhill. I had no alternative but to lay off workers and increase rents, it was the only way I could stay solvent. God knows what will happen if I lose my flock of closewools."

At this point Mr Rendall called to the men working in the yard and whatever he said made them spring into action. They rescued over forty ewes and housed them safely in the barn, by which time Tom had recovered enough to go and check them over.

Mr Rendall used his tractor to make sure Tom got home safely. I declined a lift hoping the crisp air would clear my head.

Thanks to some vicious easterly winds, the snow drifts formed again and again, and most of the children could not return to school until half-term. Jack Beam, our village headmaster, opened Ashenridge primary for those who could walk there, but he found himself labouring under great difficulties with frozen water and a shortage of fuel for the stoves. I kept token services going at Ashenridge while Roy did the same at Westaleigh, but there was no hope of getting to Brookworthy or Combe Peter, the two other churches in our care.

It was an unforgettable moment when the power and telephone cables were restored. Sadly, one of my first calls brought news of the death of old Mrs Powley who lived on the outskirts of Ashenridge. Due to the atrocious weather her funeral had to be delayed, which further deepened Albert Powley's despair. He lost the will to live, and a few weeks later I laid him to rest beside his wife.

The great winter of 1962-1963 will never be forgotten. Inevitably it created many problems, but everyone pulled together. Old arguments were forgotten – at least for a while – and new friendships were forged. A real sense of community spirit entered our lives, and those who were old enough to remember said it reminded them of the Second World War.

The strange thing is I never actually apologised to the Hawkes family for my blunder. Somehow I didn't need to. The baptism of Andrew Hawkes took place just after Easter. Little Billy Hawkes, whose prayers for snow had been answered so dramatically, fidgeted non-stop in his uncomfortable blue suit, but the service was a truly happy one and I was pleasantly surprised to see the Rendalls there. I hadn't seen Mr Rendall since Tom's accident and as we gathered in the village hall afterwards he took me to one side.

"Us got 'Awkes all wrong, rector. Never knowed the truth till 'e told us that day. Missus and I seed 'ow us'd got things all backsy-foward 'bout 'im. I suppose some good comed out of all our troubles. As 'er said to me when poor old 'Awkes sat there in our kitchen, "'Tiddn' all bad.""

Chapter 3

Birdbaths and Angels

The snow which had been beating relentlessly against our windows earlier that evening turned to rain. The cold was losing its grip.

The next day was gloriously sunny. Birds sang and spring was in the air. Bathed in the noon-day sun, the vast blanket of snow began to melt.

At Laburnum Lodge, Mrs Batchelor now had a perfect excuse to wear one of her beautiful hats which, like her, were large and lovely. She was in seventh heaven wandering among the spring flowers. She'd always considered Ashenridge churchyard an extension of her own garden, and as she stood gazing at it glorious pictures of its transformation filled her head. She was planning yet another surprise for the rector.

The sunshine that day, magnificent though it was, brought me back to the normal routine of parish life. The run up to Christmas, followed by the harshest winter known for many years, had meant that for a while peace reigned in all four parishes in the Badger Group. Even Peter Eastridge had called off his anti-Longfield campaign. Six years on he was still angry that I hadn't automatically made him churchwarden when his father died. Instead, I had insisted on a proper election for the post, as a result of which Will Swift had been elected. Unlike Peter, Will was a regular worshipper, so I felt the position had gone to the right man.

As he got older, Peter Eastridge looked more and more like his father. With a ruddy complexion and pronounced nose, he resembled a cross cockatoo, and to add to this impression his ruffled-up hair formed a crest. He never ceased trying to turn people against me. He spread rumours about my supposedly wanting to close churches. He made a fuss when the cars parked for a group service made it difficult for him to drive his tractor through the village. On another occasion he got the local newspaper to refer to me as the 'Ripping Rector' for removing pews from the back of the church. Luckily for me his plans usually backfired.

Like most of the parishioners, Mrs Batchelor was only too pleased that some of the pews had been removed. She glowed with pride every time she saw the alterations she'd paid for at the back of the church. We now had a special Sunday School area, plus wash basin and toilet, all of which had been blessed by the bishop at the official launch of the Badger Group.

Mrs Batchelor remained a great fan of mine and delighted in trying to please me. Unfortunately, her 'surprises' had a habit of landing me in hot water.

Knowing that I often went into church early to pray, Mrs Batchelor just happened to be passing as I came through the lychgate. She called to me in her fruity voice: "Rector, how wonderful the churchyard looks. That man from Brookworthy looks after it so well." Then drawing my attention to an untidy corner near the gate, she shook her head and continued. "But what a pity he can't get his mower in there." She pointed to some coarse grass. "It looks so untidy. Would you mind if I replaced it with a couple of evergreen shrubs?"

I should have known better. Give Mrs Batchelor an inch and she'd usually take a yard!

When I told Mary about it she was uneasy. "Be careful, Jack. Remember the incident with the red curtains at Ashenridge Church."

With the improved weather, and more than one church to serve, I decided to take week-day prayers at the three other churches in the Badger Group. It was Roy's turn to take the Sunday service at Ashenridge which meant I wouldn't be there for several days.

I was working in the study when the phone rang. The voice at the other end was so deafening I had to hold the receiver at arm's length. There was no mistaking Peter Eastridge's angry voice. He wanted to know what on earth had happed to his uncle's grave? I started to explain that I hadn't been in the churchyard for a few days and would go and take a look immediately, but he slammed the phone down before I'd finished speaking.

I could see at a glance what had upset him. If Mrs Batchelor had wanted to give me a surprise she'd certainly succeeded. As promised, the ugly coarse grass had been removed and evergreen shrubs planted in one corner, but standing slap bang in the middle of a nearby mound was a stone birdbath, its base surrounded by multi-coloured polyanthus. A wooden cross stood beside it with the words 'for our dear feathered friends' carved on it.

I had no alternative but to go straight round to Mrs Batchelor and tell her the distress she'd caused. She listened carefully as I went on to explain why the family was so upset. Being such a good-natured and gracious lady she promised that by the end of the day the mound would look just as it had before.

I'm afraid 'gracious' was hardly the word to describe Peter Eastridge when I called to see him later that morning. "'Tis no good now, 'arm's been done."

Determined to ignore my explanation, Peter's voice grew louder and louder. "The 'arm's been done. Fancy that daft old bat making poor uncle look some gurt fool. Puttin' flowers and a birdbath on 'im. 'Tis a ruddy disgrace. The old fool's mad and 'er 'as far too much say 'bout what 'appens in church. 'Twas 'er that made you get rid of our family pew for 'er Sunday School – never even asked me. 'Er's always stirring things up and us knows why 'er gets away with 'un. Why, you'm livin' out of 'er pocket. Everybody knows 'er sends you Christmas 'ampers."

There was no reasoning with him, so I quickly walked away and left him yelling at the top of his voice: "You mark my words, you 'aven' 'eard the last of this."

On market day Peter Eastridge was holding court in the Leighford Arms telling everyone about the rector's terrible act of desecration. "'E put a birdbath on poor old uncle's grave an' put all they mamsy pamsy flowers round it. Even worse, 'e added a sign sayin' 'twas for our dear feathered friends."

This last remark didn't have quite the effect Peter had expected and his audience burst out laughing, remembering that years ago his uncle had been a beater with the local pheasant shoot *and* an occasional poacher.

At the other end of the bar Martin Lane could hardly believe his ears. He left the pub distraught and with tears in his eyes. He was deeply hurt about his little daughter, Sarah, who'd died less than a year ago. Not for her a birdbath, the rector wouldn't even allow an angel on her grave. What was it the rector had said? Something about church officials only allowing simple headstones now because cherubs and angels got stained and disfigured by the weather.

"Did you say the rector put a birdbath on a grave?" Jean Lane couldn't believe what her husband had just said. "It isn't fair. He told us we couldn't have an angel on little Sarah's grave. Our poor little maid who only lived four months. Come on Martin, we'll have our say at the rectory. I'll give that two-faced rector what for."

Perhaps it was our good fortune that Mary and I happened to be shopping in Whiteminster that afternoon because, finding no one at home, Jean and Martin decided to go in search of the birdbath. They searched in vain – Mrs Batchelor had kept her word.

As always, their daughter's grave was a mass of white and gold flowers, and as she stood there Jean began sobbing uncontrollably at the loss of her child. She thought of what might have been, and refused to accept the injustice of it all.

From her nearby garden Annie Cooke heard a woman crying, and with a mixture of curiosity and genuine concern walked across to the churchyard. Jean and Martin were staring at a grave adorned with a weeping angel.

Through her tears Jean asked her husband: "Why won't he let us have something like that for our Sarah?"

Before he could reply, Annie was alongside them. "Sad, isn't it, the death of a child? The saddest thing of all."

The Lanes didn't seem a bit surprised to see Annie there. She continued: "I know a churchyard not far from here with one just like that." Annie pointed to the weeping angel. "My sister's little girl, Jenny. Only three when she was killed in a dreadful accident. I loved her like she was my own. That was years ago. No rules about gravestones then. The mason made an angel to go on her grave and it was beautiful, just like Jenny."

Anticipating Annie's full support, Martin was about to say: "Told you so," but Annie hadn't finished.

"It was beautiful, but every time I looked at it I got so upset. In the end I couldn't go there. That was years ago, but one day quite recently I felt I must go back and take one more look. I wish I hadn't. Her beautiful face had been cracked by the frost and blackened with age. I'll never forget it."

A tearful Annie wandered back home leaving behind her two figures deep in thought.

Jean and Martin called at the rectory the following morning. "Mr Longfield, we've changed our minds about the gravestone. Perhaps it'll be best for little Sarah if we have the one you suggested."

Chapter 4

Spode Cups and Frontals

"Why, rector, 'tis the Wilkinson family pew," I was informed by Mrs Way, the long-standing cleaner of Brookworthy Church. "I always likes to keep it well polished, just in case they comes. Only 'tis a pity when it rains, the roof leaks just there," she added.

"Do you know, I don't think I've ever seen any of them sit in that pew," I observed.

The roof at Brookworthy Church leaked every time it rained, and the severe winter had made matters worse. Fund raising for repairs seemed to be getting nowhere, so I didn't hesitate when Mrs Wilkinson invited me to the farm to receive a gift for the church. Anything would be welcome towards the roof fund.

A brightly-shining kettle sang away on the hot plate of the Rayburn. Mrs Wilkinson sat in state at one end of the table, her rosy cheeks half-hidden by curly grey hair. Her unmarried daughters, Laura and Nora, sat side by side on the opposite side of the table.

Tea was poured from a silver teapot into beautiful blue Spode cups which normally lived in a glass-fronted display cabinet. They only saw the light of day on special occasions and apparently this was one of them. Delicious home-made seed cake was served on matching plates.

"Mr Longfield, I'm going to give you a little present today. It's a cheque for £50."

Two pairs of spectacles glinted as the girls nodded in agreement.

"It's for something very special for the church," Mrs Wilkinson continued. The girls nodded again. In fact Laura and Nora nodded in agreement with everything their mother said.

I was just about to thank them, and say how badly we needed money for the roof fund, when Mrs Wilkinson continued.

"I've always wanted to give something in memory of my dear husband and the girls tell me you have a bare altar table at Brookworthy. This money is for new frontals."

My heart sank. Brookworthy Church already had a perfectly good set of frontals. What she had called a 'bare altar' was in fact a fine Jacobean table. Instead of covering it, the frontals now hung on the wall behind. Lighting had been cleverly focused on them giving greater prominence to the magnificent old altar table.

I was struggling to find the right words when Ted Hobbs, their workman, cried for help. Some sheep had broken out on to the road. By the time we'd retrieved them I was running late for another appointment and had to leave rather abruptly.

Why was it, I wondered, that whenever the church had a problem people donated something that had little or nothing to do with it. Mrs Wilkinson had not actually given me the cheque so I had good reason to return to the farm. Perhaps I could steer the subject round to the leaking roof on my next visit.

Mr Axenham, the churchwarden at Brookworthy, was incensed when I told him what they were planning. He had no patience with the Wilkinson family, who rarely came to church anyway.

"They'm always been a queer lot. Know what, they 'ad poor old Mr Wilkinson incarcerated. 'Ad to go all the way to Bristol. Why, 'twas all wrong."

I wondered what terrible crime poor Mr Wilkinson had committed to deserve such punishment, then realised he was talking about cremation, something almost unheard of in villages round here at that time.

This cast a new light on things. Assuming the ashes had been scattered and not buried, the Wilkinson family had no grave to visit, nowhere to place flowers, and no tangible memorial to a much-loved man. This explained why the family wanted to give a specific object to the church by which to remember him. They must have been discussing it for the last ten years.

Mr Axenham insisted, "'Tis mad wastin' £50 on things the church don't want when the roof be leakin' like a calendar."

My next visit to the Wilkinson farm was almost a carbon copy of the first. Out came the Spode cups and saucers, out came the matching plates with one slice of seed cake for each of us. On went the nodding heads. Was this a good moment to introduce the subject of the leaking roof?

Before I could say a word Mrs Wilkinson asked, "Have you bought the frontals yet?" Three faces looked at me expectantly across the table.

I had to explain that the Church Council and the Diocese would have to agree before any changes could be made. Their faces fell. I explained about the discovery of the Jacobean altar and why there was no need to cover the table. Their faces fell further.

"It's that man Axenham's fault. He's upset the whole parish. Ruined the church." Laura and Nora nodded in agreement with their mother.

Somehow I felt this would be the last time I got the Spode treatment. Mrs Wilkinson glowered at me. "Well, Mr Longfield, I think there's only one thing for it. You'd better return the cheque and we'll leave it at that."

"But I don't have the cheque."

"I gave you a cheque for £50," she retorted.

Laura and Nora nodded.

"When did you give it to me?" I asked.

"When you first came here." Mrs Wilkinson's rosy cheeks were turning purple. "Call yourself a man of God. I think you'd better leave."

I made as dignified an exit as I could. Ted Hobbs was emerging from one of the farm buildings. Poor Ted. Everybody regarded him as a bit of a miserable old churl, but after the treatment I'd just received I felt a good deal of sympathy for him.

Hand on heart, I knew Mrs Wilkinson hadn't given me the cheque, but all the same Mary and I hunted high and low for it.

Later that evening I slipped into the Coach and Horses. The only other person in the bar was Jim 'for what it's worth' Stillman. Jim had always been dismissive about the church, but we got on well enough.

"Here, rector," he said seriously, "I want to talk to you about something."

For a moment I wondered if the Wilkinson ladies had been spreading gossip about me, but I was wrong. Jim held up a copy of the Badger Group parish magazine.

"Look, on page 17, you tell us we ought to give our money to missionaries in Africa. Huh, missionaries! When we all know the people who really need it are the starving in India. Fine idea that is, lining the pockets of prosperous European missionaries while the natives are dying. Come off it, rector, you can do better than that. That's the church for you!"

"Last time I came in here you were holding forth about churches making grants to freedom fighters, or guerrillas as you called them. You can't have it both ways, Jim. The money is for missions, not just missionaries, and they are usually the best people to make sure our donations go to feed the hungry."

"Get on," he continued, now beginning to enjoy the banter "We all know what the church gets up to!"

"And delivery men," I added. "We all know what they get up to. Off to their fancy women, all in the firm's time and on the firm's petrol!"

By now three others had joined in the fun. A red-faced Jim was trying, unsuccessfully, to convince them he did not spend all his time visiting shapely blondes. I winked at him. "Tell you what, Jim, it takes an honest man like you to make sure we don't get overcharged for our deliveries. You're straight and I'd stand up for you anywhere...for what it's worth!"

The laughter continued, and as I made my way to the door I bumped into Ted Hobbs. Although he worked for the Wilkinsons in Brookworthy his home was in Ashenridge and he was a regular at the Coach and Horses, often stopping by for a drink on his way home. Miserable by nature he might be, but I didn't think he was the sort to pass on tittle-tattle – indeed he rarely said much. As we passed each other he simply shrugged and shook his head.

Mary was about to serve supper when a rather apologetic sergeant from Leighford Police Station called. "I'm sorry, Mr Longfield, I'm only doing my duty. Mrs Wilkinson's made allegations about you taking her £50 cheque so I had to make enquiries."

He wanted to know about any recent dealings at the bank and I quickly showed him my paying in book. He seemed happy with this and as he walked back to his car I could clearly hear him whistling one of my favourite Gilbert & Sullivan songs:

'When constabulary duty's to be done, to be done
A policeman's lot is not an 'appy one, 'appy one'

I was more than relieved the constable had believed me, but then the phone rang and it was Ray, the landlord at the Coach and Horses, asking if I could pop in for a few minutes. What was I going to find there, some sort of 'kangaroo court' with Peter Eastridge sitting in the seat of judgment? That £50 cheque had become more trouble than it was worth.

Ray nodded towards the end of the bar where Ted Hobbs was perched on his familiar stool.

"Sorry to drag yer out, Mr Longfield, but don' tek no notice of they," he said in a deep voice. "They'm all mazed. They'm all as bad. The old 'un says it, and they maids does whatever 'er says."

"What are you trying to tell me, Ted?"

"'Tis all lies 'bout you. 'Er just 'magines it. Tried it on me over me pay sayin' they'd done 'un when they 'adn'. I walked out there and then. They comed rushin' after me. I says I wasn' goin' to be talked to like that. The old scarecrow sets they off, and they all goes screechin'."

Poor Ted. I wondered why he bothered to stay with them.

"One day 'er's goin' to find that there cheque, an' then they'll be all sweet agin."

Jim and the others at the bar could hardly pretend they weren't listening. Everybody wanted to be in on the story. It hadn't been my intention to broadcast my troubles to one and all, but now the story was out I wanted them to hear my version.

"I think I've got an idea." Jim sounded excited. "You know I'm no churchman, but I'm no heathen either. In fact it may surprise you to know that I enjoy looking round churches."

"So that's where you take the van," someone joked.

"And who do you meet?"

There were laughs all round.

"No. It isn't like that," Jim protested. "For what it's worth, I like looking at old buildings. Not so long ago I was talking to one of these parsons and he told me a similar story about people wanting to give useless things to the church when the whole place was falling down. So he had an idea. He bought a beautiful book and inside it he recorded the names of those in whose memory donations were made. Then the money was used where it was most needed. He never had a problem again."

"They old fools'll never do that, they'll never put their names in a book," scoffed Ted.

"Perhaps not," Jim replied, "But they might give the book." "They'll have to find the cheque first," I added. "I hate to think what they'd do to me if I came up with that idea right now."

A few weeks later fire engines could be heard racing through the village in the middle of the night. A fire had started in one of the bedrooms at the Wilkinson farmhouse. The women were badly shaken but otherwise unharmed, which was more than could be said for the farmhouse. The fire brigade saved most of the roof, but inevitably there was a lot of water damage.

Normally I would have called and offered to help, but I found myself hesitating. The Wilkinsons didn't trust me and I might make matters worse. I waited until seven o'clock that evening and slipped into the Coach and Horses knowing I'd find Ted there. I enquired how things were on the farm.

"Middlin'."

"Does anyone know what caused the fire?"

"Can't say."

"Do you think they'd let me help if I called?"

There was a sharp intake of breath and he shook his head.

Conversation with Ted had clearly dried up so I joined in the chat with the others at the bar. After a few minutes Ted finished his pint, then turning to Ray said, "I'll 'ave me usual to take 'ome."

To my surprise he produced some crisp new banknotes and was handed a bottle of whisky. Looking straight at me, he slipped the bottle into his raincoat pocket. "There, that'll travel best like that till tomorrow mornin'." Then giving me another knowing look he added, "I 'spect the old scarecrow won't mind seein' you after that."

What on earth did he mean?

The farm looked a sorry sight. Most of the roof was covered in tarpaulins, the cob walls were smoke stained and the cobbled yard was full of blackened furniture. Ted was filling a builder's lorry and I went to give him a hand.

"You can take they," he said, pointing to a large cardboard box.

It was damp, and as I lifted it on to the lorry the bottom gave way. Bottle after bottle slid to the ground. Whisky bottles. So that was it! I started throwing them into the lorry one at a time and as I did so Mrs Wilkinson appeared in the yard. Ted was right. With her unkempt hair, ashen face and heavily rouged cheeks she looked like a scarecrow. The fire had certainly knocked the stuffing out of her.

I stood there, a bottle in each hand, not knowing what to say. She looked from me to the bottles. "A drop of whisky never did anyone any harm, Mr Longfield."

If she called that a drop I dreaded to think what a lot looked like!

According to the death certificate, Mrs Wilkinson died of a heart attack. I thought 'alcoholic poisoning' might have been nearer the mark. She was buried in Brookworthy churchyard on one of the wettest days of the month, and Laura and Nora discovered just how damp it could be sitting in the family pew. Ted Hobbs and Mr Axenham sat two rows behind. There were only a few other mourners.

41

Memories of the £50 cheque had grown dim until I received a call from Laura and Nora Wilkinson, and as I set out for their farm I wondered what lay behind such an unexpected invitation.

I turned off the open ridge road and drove by lush woodlands before dipping down towards Brookworthy. Gold, yellow and rich-red leaves came drifting down from the trees carpeting the road ahead of me.

The farmhouse had been completely restored and the girls led me into a spotless kitchen. Laura kept fidgeting with a copy of the *Good Housekeeping Cookery Book* and made a point of showing me a recipe for seed cake. As she did so a piece of paper fluttered on to the table. Both girls were full of apologies and explained that it was only when they decided to make seed cake again that the cheque had come to light. Their mother must have left it there by mistake. Laura pressed the cheque into my hand.

Having overcome their embarrassment, Laura and Nora began talking about giving something tangible to the church in memory of their parents. Sitting in the Wilkinson pew on the day of their mother's funeral they'd had first-hand experience of the leaking roof – much to Mr Axenham's delight! They were thinking along the lines of a leather-bound book to record the names of those in whose memory donations had been made to the church. The donations could then be used wherever needed. They admitted the idea had come from someone else. I knew straight away who that someone was.

The brightly shining kettle was singing its head off. Out came the silver teapot, out came the Spode cups and saucers, and as we enjoyed the freshly-baked seed cake three heads nodded in perfect harmony.

Chapter 5

Every Picture Tells a Story

In a way I'd seen the whole thing at a glance, but it was a long time before I appreciated the significance of what I was looking at.

In the centre of the painting was the figure of a young woman kneeling by a stream, her long hair almost touching the water, her graceful hands spread out on a pebbled shore. She looked sad and lonely. The same mood was echoed in the grey rocks which surrounded her, and the dark cloudy sky. The whole picture was framed by the branch of a weeping willow tree.

Since Mary had started attending art classes I'd visited several exhibitions, and there was certainly a fair amount of local talent. For some reason I could not get this one painting out of my mind.

In a way it reflected my own mood that summer's afternoon. Roy Edwards, my first curate, had just left Westaleigh for another parish. Although I'd had many a battle with Roy in the early days, he'd eventually overcome his impatience with what seemed to him the impossibly slow ways of the Church of

England, and had achieved so much during his three years curacy. He and his wife, Lucy, would be sadly missed.

Roy's strength had undoubtedly been his work with the younger members of the parish. The youth club he'd started now totalled fifty members – an amazing number for a remote rural area and one of the benefits of the four parishes in the Badger Group working together. He'd organised a hugely successful Holiday Club at Brookworthy during the Whitsun half-term which brought in almost every child in the parish, more than we could ever have hoped for.

It came as a great blow when the bishop announced he needed Roy elsewhere to lead a team ministry. Despite my protests, he insisted that any curate should spend only three years training with me. He was already finding it difficult attracting younger men to work in rural parishes, and it was my role to give them sufficient training to do just that.

Roy's successor, Cedric Palmer, would not have been my first choice. Aged twenty-seven, he'd studied at Cambridge and finally trained at a well-known Anglican theological college. I would have preferred a married couple, but he relished the idea of setting up home alone at Westaleigh Vicarage and made it clear he was a confirmed bachelor.

Tall, dark-haired and bespectacled, he had quite a distinguished appearance for one so young. The churchwardens took to him instantly. At Ashenridge, Colonel Waters described him as 'capital company'. Will Swift was pleased to hear he was musical, and hoped he would continue with the Badger Group Choir which Lucy Edwards had run so successfully. At Westaleigh, Sir William Radlett claimed 'he's just the sort of chap we are looking for', whilst dear old Tom

Short, very much a traditionalist, was delighted that Cedric had shown so much interest in church buildings.

There had to be a fly in the ointment, and I soon discovered what that was. Cedric was completely out of his depth with young people. The Friday evening youth club degenerated into a riot which he came to dread. I tried to help, but numbers were falling and Cedric kept finding more and more excuses to cancel Friday evening activities

At one of our regular Monday meetings Cedric confided in me. He'd spent most of that weekend praying for a solution, and a couple of days later it looked as though his prayers had been answered. With the arrival of the morning post had come a letter announcing a meeting to be held in Leighford aimed specifically at helping church youth workers.

At my suggestion Cedric went to the meeting. He called in at the rectory the following morning, beaming all over his face. He'd met someone by the name of Nick Hall, a youth worker who'd recently moved to Leighford to take up a new job. Nick had been hoping to find a local group to work with and Cedric asked if it would be OK to bring him round to meet me the following evening.

A slim, energetic man, in his early forties, I was not surprised to learn Nick had been a sergeant major. Sadly, he and his wife, Jane, were unable to have children, which was why he loved working with them.

Much to Cedric's relief, and mine, Nick took over the youth club. I agreed to this on the clear understanding that Cedric would join him every Friday evening, both to support him and learn from him. His first curacy was, after all, rather like an apprenticeship.

Things went like a bomb. Instead of having an unscheduled programme with occasional events, everything was planned from start to finish. The re-vamped youth club was to have football and netball teams with cricket and tennis in the summer. Instructors would be coming to talk about first aid, life saving and survival, the latter in preparation for a thirty-six hour trek over the moor.

A committee of parents, with representatives from the youngsters, was formed, and Nick persuaded a local farmer to let us have the use of one of his fields for outdoor activities.

Everyone was enthusiastic until they realised exactly what was involved. The first shock wave to hit the four parishes came with Nick's demand for home-made cakes, jams and pies, plus home-grown vegetables and plants – anything that could be sold at his Summer Fund Raiser. Next, he wanted people to collect dozens of prizes for the tombola. And, of course, help would be needed to decorate the parish hall. The list was growing longer by the minute.

As the big day approached Nick went into overdrive. Anyone who showed the slightest hesitation in supporting his plans was told very firmly 'We owe it to our children. If we can't do our best for them we might as well give up'.

Some parents detected that Nick might resign and, remembering the chaos before he arrived, went along with his demands.

The Summer Fund Raiser – or SFR as it had come to be known – raised well over £75, and on the back of its success

Nick immediately swung into action and began making plans for another event.

Heather Small was a poor reader, and her teacher at Leighford Secondary Modern was worried that she was falling behind with her work. Mr & Mrs Small blamed the youth club. Having spent many hours making cakes and handicrafts for the SFR, she was now expected to go to the hall after school once or twice a week for netball practice to make sure of a place in the team.

I invited Nick over for a drink. I think he guessed why. "You know, Nick, you're doing a fantastic job with our youngsters. Perhaps too good a job. I've had a complaint from Heather Small's parents – did you know she's been falling behind with her school work?"

At the mention of Heather, Nick started fidgeting and accused me of listening to tittle-tattle. "I don't see how you can be critical. I give the youth club my all, morning, noon and night. What about the mess you and Cedric made of it. Quite frankly, I think it's time you looked for another leader."

This wasn't quite what I'd expected and I asked him to think things over before doing anything hasty.

Later that week Mrs Small rang. Was I aware that Nick had been helping Heather with her reading? What was more, he was planning to give her a key part in the next youth service.

I now discovered this was just one of the many occasions when Nick went out of his way to help. He spent a lot of time showing one boy how to stand up against being bullied at school. He sat for hours by the bedside of another lad recovering from a road accident. He showed infinite patience with a handicapped girl until she learnt the skill of catching a ball.

As time went by the youngsters became devoted to him, and it was they who silenced their parents if they complained about Nick's demands.

Although Nick had won the hearts of the children, and some of the parents, others saw him in a very different light. There was a major fuss when he refused to change the date of his autumn sale which clashed with the one at Westaleigh. Next, he nearly came to blows with the mums over the food they should serve their offspring at the Christmas party. Finally, the festivities at Ashenridge Church almost came to a halt when he demanded that we sing some modern carols at the combined Sunday School and Youth Carol Service. To cap it all, he insisted that the choir sat with the congregation so that his performers could use their stalls.

One evening in March he came to me in an awful stew because some of the boys from the farms had refused to turn out. These included his best football players.

I let him vent his feelings then pointed out that it was the lambing season, and the boys were either too busy or too tired, or both. Then I threw a key question at him – how did his wife cope now that he was out almost every night of the week? He winced. How much time did they actually spend together? Hardly any time at all. Even on Sundays they seemed to go their separate ways.

"But don't you want to spend more time together?" I asked.

He winced again. "Jane doesn't have time for me. She doesn't understand...."

I seemed to be getting nowhere with Nick and asked Mary how she would feel if she was his wife?

Until that evening Mary hadn't even known her first name, but when I said 'Jane Hall' Mary exclaimed, "I wonder if it's the same Jane in my art class. She joined last summer. Do you remember her painting in the exhibition, the one of the woman by the stream who looked so sad?"

Mary hesitated and gave me a thoughtful look. "I wouldn't like it at all, Jack, but I suppose it's easier for us because we're involved in so many things in the parish that bring us together anyway."

I dreamt about the painting that night and recognised Jane as the lonely figure by the stream. I saw Nick coming home, exhausted after yet another evening at the youth club. Nick and Jane might live under the same roof, but I wondered how often they actually met up with each other.

During the summer term several parents pressed us to organise another Holiday Club. The one organised by my previous curate had been a huge success, but it did require an awful lot of hard work. To begin with Nick refused to get involved. Even he realised he couldn't keep things going for a whole week – after all he had a full-time job to think about. But after repeated requests he reconsidered and came to us with an idea. At the beginning of the school holidays, why not put on a Youth Gala and invite other groups to join in? It would be something for everyone to enjoy.

We agreed, but I suspected there might be a price to pay. Even as we spoke I could picture Nick going into overdrive again. A period of chaos lay ahead.

Anyone who had their wits about them kept well out of Nick's way as Saturday the 25th July drew near. Three other groups were involved, and a tournament between the teams included netball, football and other sporting events.

Before things had even got started Nick had a row with the youth club leaders because they hadn't filled in his forms properly. This was largely thanks to his ambiguous instructions, but of course Nick couldn't see that. Then there was a major fuss over refreshments. When Nick spoke about providing lunch he meant a cooked meal, but the mums thought he meant a cold buffet. To make matters worse the winning teams scoffed most of the food before the others got a look in.

All this was bad enough, but it paled into insignificance when the Youth Gala Service in Ashenridge Church started the following morning. Nick arrived early and discovered that Mrs Batchelor had filled the church with flowers. He definitely did not want flowers at this particular service and hurled them into an overgrown corner of the churchyard.

A row then broke out with the organist over the hymns because Nick had forgotten to give him a list beforehand. Once again the choir found itself dismissed from the stalls and the whole service was performed in a very modern format.

Undoubtedly the most difficult aspect of the service was the play – a modern version of the Good Samaritan. Instead of a poor wounded traveller, Nick's version portrayed a drunken layabout who'd been thrown out of a pub. The boy playing the part staggered about before finally collapsing on to the stage. His acting was a bit too realistic for some. Then a solicitor went past in a chauffeur-driven car, followed by a clergyman who had no intention of stopping to help because he was in too much of a hurry to get to church. I had an unpleasant feeling this last character was supposed to be me.

Finally, one of our club members, a well-known extrovert, took the part of a tough motorcyclist, dressed from head to toe in leathers. The point about this man caring for the drunkard may have been well portrayed, but it was lost on most of the audience who were shocked by his crude gestures and bad language.

After the service Nick was shunned by the audience – most of them had hated the service and were still unhappy about the traumas of the previous day. Nick's interpretation of the Good Samaritan had certainly got everyone talking, but for all the wrong reasons.

Not surprisingly Nick came round to see me. He was in a terrible state saying everyone had let him down, and now they were blaming him for what went wrong. Nobody listened to what he was saying. People simply did not appreciate all the time he had put into the event, an event the youngsters of today could actually identify with. He'd never come across such an ungrateful crowd of old fossils – and the clergy were no better. This last comment was aimed firmly in my direction. Oh dear, was Nick on the point of resigning, again?

He was anxious to get away, but I stopped him and asked what he was planning to do now – go home and spend his time stewing over matters and feeling sorry for himself? How would his wife cope with that? As he made for the door I risked a parting shot and asked him where his previous youth work had ended? He looked embarrassed – I knew I'd touched a raw nerve. I reminded him of all the good he had done and the greater things he would achieve if only he became less impatient and stopped letting his temper get the better of him.

Nick sat down. "The the people here would never work with me again, would they?"

"No, not if you go on as you have in the past. You've achieved so much, but you go about things in the wrong way. I've heard you're working wonders with the firm you set up in Leighford. Why can't you use the same approach with the people here?"

Nick remained silent.

"Look, I know you don't really want to give up the youth club. Why not take a break and spend some time with Jane? You owe it to her. I'll try to pick up the pieces here, and it's about time Cedric started pulling his weight."

Ashenridge Church Council was due to meet a few days after the Gala. This was normally a run-of-the-mill meeting to fix the autumn programme, but when someone mentioned the words 'Gala Service' it was like a dam being breached and the complaints came flooding out.

"There's only one thing to do with that youth leader. Sack him."

"I think the play was disgraceful. I've never heard such language. It's just the sort of thing we don't want to hear in church."

"I've sung in the choir for over twenty years and that wretched man thinks he can simply throw us out. If he stays on that's the last you'll see of me."

"I've never been so badly treated. I spent hours cooking pasties, and that mini-Hitler said he didn't like them. He actually expected us to make a roast lunch on those gas rings in the hall."

"And let's not forget poor Mrs Batchelor's flowers. She went to such a lot of trouble and that awful man threw them aside. There's no doubt about it, he'll have to go."

Then Mrs Batchelor spoke. "I must confess I was hurt when I saw what had happened to my beautiful flowers. I nearly walked out, but I felt we must try to support our young ones, no matter how badly their leader behaved. Being a little deaf, I found it hard to follow some of the service, but I have never heard the children sing so well. They put everything into it. Like others here tonight, I felt distinctly uncomfortable when the children started their sketch of the Good Samaritan. It was all too modern for me. But I went home thinking about some of the complaints made about Mr Hall, complaints I'd readily agreed with, and I began to feel ashamed."

There was no doubting Mrs Batchelor's sincerity and as she continued all eyes were fixed on her.

"When you think about it, Mr Hall isn't unlike that man by the roadside, yet here we are throwing him out of the church, just like the drunk who was thrown out of the pub. Respectable churchgoers like us are simply passing him by, treating him with contempt. The motorcyclist wasn't that different from a lot of the children in our towns and villages today. Above all, I believe it would be wrong of us to forget that many of our children are all the better for knowing Mr Hall."

She, more than anyone, had good reason to feel hurt, and her words made everyone think again. The atmosphere in the hall lightened and other members of the council spoke up remembering the great pains to which Nick had gone to help their children, and indeed grandchildren.

That October Mary's art class organised another exhibition. Once again I was drawn to one particular painting, a watercolour of a man and a woman gazing across a stream to distant green hills. The man had his arm curled lovingly around the woman's shoulder; a brilliant sun shone down on them from a cloudless blue sky.

I did not need to look at the signature – I knew who'd painted it.

Chapter 6

Friendship

"Oh, Jack, I haven't laughed like that for ages." Mary had just arrived home from her art class and could hardly speak for giggling. "Stephanie's great fun and we've become such good friends, and it's lovely that Paul and Ann get on so well with their children. Stephanie reckons you and I need to relax with friends a bit more often. They'd like us to have lunch with them soon. You know it would do us both a power of good."

Mary was right. Apart from church and family activities we rarely went out. This was partly due to my theological training where we were discouraged from getting too close to our parishioners for fear of being accused of having 'favourites'. So I left it to Mary to make all the arrangements and genuinely looked forward to meeting Stephanie and Henry Burrows.

While we waited for the door to be opened I looked up at the house. It had a porch with a stone archway, similar to a church. The ancient timbers supporting the roof were carved with a leaf pattern. The letters 'HB' stood out clearly on the huge wooden lintel over the door. I was wondering what this meant when Henry Burrows opened the door. He was a tall man, I guessed in his forties, with a warm friendly face and a twinkle in his eyes. We got on like a house on fire and soon discovered we had a common interest in history. While Stephanie was showing Mary some of her paintings, Henry gave me a grand tour of the house. The 'HB' above the door stood for another Henry Burrows, one of his forbears. The Burrows family had farmed there since the sixteenth century. The family history continued as we went up and down passages and carefully negotiated crooked steps. I admired huge fireplaces, dark oak panelling, unusual wood carvings and ancient plastered ceilings.

Mary offered to help Stephanie with the lunch and I could hear them laughing together. Henry was keen to tell me about an amazing find on the farm – a very old earthenware jug had been discovered when they were digging out a new drain. Having been restored it now had pride of place on the mantelpiece. I followed Henry's gaze. It was hardly a thing of beauty.

Henry went to help in the kitchen and suggested I might like to take a closer look at the jug. I lifted it up carefully, but before I had a chance to inspect it the jug came away from the handle and broke into pieces on the stone hearth. I was left holding the handle, at which point Henry came back into the room. He looked from the broken jug to me. I blurted out my apologies and bent to pick up the pieces. One had the letters 'poo' incised on it. Another bore the letters 'esen'. I fitted the fragments together. 'A Present from Blackpool'.

Henry was bent double. "Oh, Jack. Look what you've done. You've ruined the precious present my cousin gave me."

Still laughing he added, "I only hope he doesn't buy me a replacement."

We were still laughing on our way home in the car. Anyone seeing us might have thought we were a little mad, but it wasn't only the incident with the jug that had amused us. We were laughing because we knew we'd made friends with the Burrows, a lovely couple with whom we could truly relax.

We became firm friends and nothing but good came of it. One day over lunch at the rectory Mary asked Stephanie what she thought of the abstract picture hanging in our dining room. It consisted of six intertwined curls painted in brightly-coloured oils and was graced with the title 'Friendship'.

Stephanie and Henry made all sorts of polite comments until our smiles gave the game away. Mary had painted it that very morning. It had taken her all of thirty minutes and was barely dry when she put it in the frame.

"Who's had the last laugh now?" I chuckled.

Not long after that I bumped into Henry at Leighford Market.

"I've just been talking to that curate of yours. Odd sort. I happened to mention carol singing and he gave me to understand he doesn't approve of it. Said the church should give to the poor, not beg from them. But I seem to remember Paul and Ann telling me that your church usually goes carol singing and most people love it. Would you let me organise something?"

This was too good an offer to refuse. "All right," I replied. "If you start with the Hartons at the far end of the parish you can work your way back towards the rectory. Paul will show you how to get there."

Two days before Christmas Henry drove a minibus along the track to Woods Cottage. One of the young mums declared, "It's no good singing carols there, they'll only put in a few pennies."

"Quite right," agreed another. "We want to make as much money as we can. We'll be wasting our time."

Henry ignored them and steered the bus along the track. Another carol singer declared, "Told you it wouldn't be any good. It's all in darkness."

"No, look," said Henry, turning off the headlights. "I think I can see a light. If we park here they won't see us until we're ready. Be careful where you shine your torches and keep quiet."

Silently the party approached the cottage. A single candle lit the room inside and through the uncurtained windows the Hartons could be seen sitting on either side of a meagre fire. Although Christmas was only two days away there were no decorations and one solitary card stood in the middle of a table.

At the first notes of 'Silent night' the couple looked up in alarm. Slowly Mrs Harton got to her feet, peered out of the window, and eventually unbolted the door. She gazed in amazement at the singers then, fumbling in her apron pocket, found two little coins which she dropped into the tin. The torchlight showed there were tears in her eyes.

"There, my love," she said softly. "Fifty years us's been 'ere, and this is the fust time as us's ever 'eard they singers. 'Tis like Christmas when us was young. Bless you my dears."

Mr Harton joined his wife in the doorway as the carollers sang 'Away in a manger'.

The story came pouring out at the rectory later that evening. Over cups of tea and mince pies everyone said they could not forget the miserable scene at Woods Cottage – especially the solitary Christmas card.

This reminded Stephanie of a man in Leighford whose working life had been cut short through ill health. Once very active, he'd become housebound, depressed and considered his life was over. Being involved in raising money for a number of charities, Stephanie had come across an excellent idea for re-making Christmas cards. The charity provided the envelopes and blank folded cards. All he had to do was cut out pictures from used cards and stick them on the new blanks. Over the years he'd made a thousand or more and his charitable work had given him a new lease of life. Stephanie was his chief salesman, carrying them with her wherever she went. With that she delved into her bag and produced a handful of cards. They were beautifully made and we all chose a favourite and wrote a greeting inside.

On their way home Henry and Stephanie made a detour and quietly pushed the cards through the letterbox at Woods Cottage.

That was Mr & Mrs Harton's last Christmas. Early in the New Year they died within a few weeks of each other. Neither of them had been ill. In their wisdom, the social services had decided they were no longer fit enough to look after themselves and should go into care. They weren't to know the devastating effect this would have. Mrs Harton had often said that the day she or her husband had to leave the cottage would be the day they'd give up. And so it was.

A distant relative asked if I would go with her to Woods Cottage to discuss the disposal of some of the belongings. In a back room we discovered an old wooden screen decorated with Christmas cards. There was no mistaking them as the ones we'd collected at the rectory. A scruffy label had been pinned to the top of the screen and on it someone had scribbled 'a present from our friends'.

Chapter 7

Charity Ends at Home

"Every time she sees me she wants to borrow something." We were having our regular Monday meeting and Cedric was complaining bitterly about one of his neighbours. At first Mavis had simply asked to borrow little things like a pudding basin or a saucepan. Then she found she had run out of salt or sugar. She always kept her promise to repay him, but Mavis hadn't only become a nuisance, she'd become an embarrassment. People were beginning to talk about her frequent visits to Westaleigh Vicarage.

A few days later Cedric had more news. Having given Mavis some tactful hints on managing her weekly groceries, she'd now moved on to borrowing furniture polish, a tin of Brasso and the carpet sweeper.

"Does her husband know she's always borrowing things from you? Do you think he keeps her short of money?" Mary could see that Cedric was finding it difficult to handle the situation and wanted to help.

Cedric honestly didn't know, but agreed it was an avenue to explore. When he got back to the vicarage there was Mavis waiting on his doorstep. She wanted to know if he was going into town and could he give her a lift? On the way to Leighford she assured Cedric that Archie was certainly generous with his money.

Two days later it was Archie's turn. He borrowed a spade, fork and wheelbarrow. Not content with that, he asked if he could borrow the motor mower. This was taking things a bit too far, but having said 'yes' to everything else Cedric didn't know how to refuse.

I warned him he must be firm. "Their garden is so overgrown your mower will hardly cope with it. What happens if it gets broken? Who'll be responsible for replacing it?"

It was high time Cedric weaned the couple off their dependence on him. They had to learn to stand on their own feet. If Cedric was finding it difficult to say 'no' perhaps he should simply avoid them whenever possible.

Cedric's great love was church buildings. Unlike most people who can pray anywhere, my new curate was happiest praying in church. 'The holy place' was how he described it. Not long after his arrival I'd taken a service at Westaleigh and found the clergy-stall knee deep in books on prayer and meditation. The cleaners were finding it difficult to keep the church tidy as he always seemed to be there, and nobody wanted to interrupt him while he was on his knees. I decided to make capital out of his interest.

For years we'd been talking about the four churches having their own guide book so I suggested he spent time on Thursdays and Fridays studying each building and gathering additional information from the library. I was confident he would enjoy this and hoped his absence on those days would help to solve the problem with Mavis and Archie.

Cedric became totally absorbed and all four parishes were looking forward to having their own guide. The first one would cover Brookworthy. Having completed a draft, Cedric decided to take one last look before producing the final text. As he approached the church Walter Briggs, an elderly farmer, was coming towards him. He, too, was keen on the old church and knew a lot of its history. Cedric was delighted when he offered to take the draft home and read it. He was even more delighted when he got a call congratulating him on his excellent work and offering to pay for the guide to be printed.

Cedric longed to see Brookworthy Church restored to its former glory and told Walter Briggs the sadness he felt when he looked at the leaking roof, spoilt timbers, peeling decorations and stained walls. How he longed to see it a truly holy place once again – the very gateway to heaven for everyone who worshipped there. Even if he did not quite follow all of this, Walter beamed in delight. Without realising it, Cedric had unwittingly fallen into a trap.

On the evening of the Brookworthy Church Council meeting Cedric joined us for supper. I warned him things might get a bit tricky when we got to the subject of the harvest produce auction – should we keep the proceeds or give them away? My curate had no doubts about it. We should give everything to Christian Aid. Only the previous Sunday he had prayed passionately about the needs of the third world. He had followed this up the following week by holding forth about the iniquities of a church that wanted to spend all the money on itself instead of helping the homeless and starving. I knew he would back my proposal regarding the auction proceeds.

Cedric was surprised to see Walter Briggs at the meeting. But I knew Walter better than most. He was the kind of Church Councillor that many clergy simply inherit. Whether or not he actually went to church seemed to matter very little to him. He was wealthy, important, and prided himself on his reputation for being generous, which was why year after year he was automatically re-elected to the Church Council. His actual attendance at meetings depended on what was on the agenda. If he knew some threatening new idea was in the air he was more than likely to turn up. When he did, he usually acted as a rallying point for all those who resisted change. He also had a good stock of homespun proverbs. By skilful use of them he nearly always got his own way at meetings. He came that evening with a definite purpose. He knew we would be discussing what to do with the money from the harvest auction.

Walter loved the sound of his own voice so it was hardly surprising that he rarely appreciated any opinion other than his own. Consequently, he was always trying to drag us back into the past. Until a few years ago the harvest gifts had been given to the cottage hospital in Leighford. Some people had questioned whether hospitals still needed this kind of help, but Walter Briggs insisted they did.

The truth had emerged a couple of years ago. As churchwarden, Mr Axenham had gone to the hospital where he was greeted by the new matron. To his disgust she picked over the boxes and selected a few choice grapes, some eggs, tomatoes and tinned fruit. She thanked him but explained it was no longer economic to ask the kitchen staff to peel vegetables. Nowadays everything arrived pre-packed and ready to cook.

The next year I suggested we should do the same as my other parishes – sell the produce and give the money to a good cause. Walter Briggs was up in arms and convinced everybody that if the hospitals did not want it then we must give it to the old people of the parish. After all 'charity begins at home'.

Unfortunately this posed a problem – whom should we class as old? The result was endless hours spent working out a list followed by the distribution of small portions of gifts to about thirty people. Not surprisingly, the following year less produce was given and a number of well-off pensioners were amused to find themselves receiving smaller parcels. One lady living in a luxury bungalow was presented with one potato, a slightly bruised apple and a pair of runner beans. The whole thing was totally absurd and those involved made it quite clear they would never do it again.

Mr Axenham enthusiastically supported my suggestion to give this year's proceeds to Christian Aid.

"'Ow can us feed so well 'ere while they'm starvin' to Africa? Us used to send our gifts to they folks in 'ospital until they didn' want it. Then 'twas the old folks round 'ere, and they didn' want 'n neither, so why don' us 'elp they that really needs it?"

"Nonsense," someone butted in. "They only give it to guerillas or waste the money on administration."

"And send expensive things out there like combine harvesters that nobody knows how to use," came another voice. People began shaking their heads in agreement.

"How about sendin' it to that missionary in India us 'elped afore?" Mrs Way was trying to support me, but her suggestion fell on stony ground.

"That's no good. People want food and clothes, not sermons and hymns."

Then Walter Briggs spoke. There was no doubt in his mind. The church should hold on to the auction money. He turned to me with the air of a profound thinker who, having considered all the arguments, has now reached his verdict. At the same time he gave an encouraging nod in Cedric's direction.

"Yes, we must keep it for the church. You know what I always say, rector..." He paused and cleared his throat, "Charity begins at home."

"Ends there, too," muttered Mr Axenham.

Walter's remarks were met with appreciative nods from most people in the room. Clearly wisdom of this sort weighed heavier than all the proverbs of Solomon, the words of Jesus, or indeed the entire teaching of the Bible.

To strengthen his case Walter now turned to Cedric. "I know this young man will agree with me. Why, only the other day he was telling me about this church being a holy place, the gateway to heaven. There's no better cause to which we can give our money."

I could not understand why Cedric had remained so silent and his face now turned the colour of a ripe tomato. I recognised the words 'holy place' and 'gateway to heaven' as those often used by Cedric and wondered what on earth was going on.

But the oracle had spoken and the debate was closed. Once again, Walter Briggs had had the last word.

After the meeting a very apologetic Cedric explained everything. It didn't take long to work out what Walter Briggs had been up to. He'd twisted my curate around his little finger.

The next Sunday Cedric was due to take the service at Brookworthy. He'd just arrived when Mr Briggs pulled up in his car, wound down the window and cheerily said he was on his way to make sure his neighbour's sheep were all right. He could have done that at any time, but justified his action by quoting another of his little proverbs: "You know what they say, Mr Palmer, 'The better the day, the better the deed'."

Cedric couldn't get over the way Walter Briggs had used him and decided to give up all work on the guides. He doubted whether his views about holy places were of any use – after all, the early Christians probably worshipped God from a mud hut. What did it matter as long as they cared for the needy.

I told him why I felt church buildings were important. People do need somewhere beautiful, not only for worship but also to learn and sometimes have their ideas challenged. That was where people like Mr Briggs missed out. When the church does its job properly it changes peoples' attitudes. It motivates them to look beyond themselves. This is the way it worked in the old days when harvest gifts were distributed to the sick and the elderly.

"Perhaps we should be giving more to the likes of Mavis and Archie. They always seem to be in need."

I'd forgotten about Cedric's neighbours and was disappointed to hear they were still borrowing from him on a regular basis. The whole thing had become a farce and I told

Cedric in no uncertain terms it was his duty to get to the bottom of it and, bless him, he did.

It transpired that Mavis and Archie were paying dearly for a misunderstanding at the start of their marriage. Mavis had been over the moon when her prosperous grandparents said they would give them a generous sum of money to help set up home. On the strength of this they bought good furniture and kitchen fittings on hire purchase, believing they would soon be able to clear the debt. But when the cheque arrived it was for a paltry £10. The young couple were devastated. Mavis couldn't turn to her parents because her father had recently been made redundant, and Archie hadn't seen his parents in years. They had no one to turn to for help.

Mavis assured Cedric that her grandparents would be reluctant to help. "The truth is, Mr Palmer, they want everyone to think they're generous, but the reality is different."

Realising she'd been disloyal, Mavis refused to tell Cedric the name of her grandparents and quickly added, "It's not that they're mean, they're careful."

In our part of the world Christmas heralds the poultry whist drive season. Each village hall takes its turn to play host and display the prizes for all to see, the largest turkeys being earmarked for the top scorers.

Although officially retired from farming, Walter Briggs was still breeding turkeys and presented a couple of them each year to Brookworthy. Although he and his wife didn't play whist they still came along to hand out the prizes. It was all part of the annual Christmas pageant.

Westaleigh's churchwarden, Tom Short, loved his whist drives. Without revealing their names, Cedric had told Tom about his neighbours who were having financial problems. It didn't take Tom long to put two and two together. He knew Walter Briggs was Mavis's grandfather and was angry that he'd been so mean.

"You 'ave to understand, Mr Palmer, Walter's set in 'is ways. 'E's got it into 'is 'ead the youngsters today 'ave it too easy."

Tom took it upon himself to pay a surprise visit to Mavis and Archie. As Cedric had hinted, their home looked pitifully short of furniture. He felt embarrassed asking them for a prize for the whist drive, and it came as no surprise when they apologised for not being able to help, but this was the opening he needed and within minutes their story came pouring out.

Tom had an evening of triumph at Brookworthy whist drive. He was the top-scoring gent and there was applause all round as Mr Briggs presented him with his prize – a turkey that looked big enough to feed the five thousand!

Before leaving the rostrum Tom turned to Walter and his wife. "'Eard you should be congratulated too. Great-grandparents, eh. What was it your Mavis said, 'A baby in May keeps the troubles away'. Think that's what 'er said. Best see for yerselves though 'cause the poor little mite won't have a 'ome to come 'ome to the way things are goin'."

The look on their faces said it all. Tom suddenly had another thought. "An' 'twouldn' do you any 'arm to give 'em one o' they turkeys when you visits 'em."

"'Tis only right they should see for theyselves," commented Tom to Cedric a few days later. "Let's 'ope they'll think on it. Trouble is, they thinks they'm generous, but their sort of charity ends at 'ome – their own 'ome."

Chapter 8

'Tis Only Nature

"Dad, please, please can we have some lambs of our own. Paul and I will look after them, we promise."

I wondered if this might be a way of solving some of Ann's problems. She was become increasingly difficult to please and creating tension at home for all of us. The only trouble was that, short of sacrificing our own lawn, we had nowhere to keep them. Ironically, the paddock running alongside our garden actually belonged to the rectory, but for years it had been let to the Heal family at Parsonage Farm.

The bent figure of old Mr Heal would appear every morning and evening – no matter what the weather he'd be there to inspect his flock. Some days he could hardly struggle across the field thanks to his arthritis.

A shy, self-effacing man, it had taken several seasons for us to get to know him and as we did he became increasingly happy to let Paul and Ann lend a hand. Sometimes they were a little less keen. Those were the days when Mr Heal might be seen going home with a dead lamb swinging at his side. Occasionally he and his son might appear with a tractor and link box to remove a dead ewe, her lambs still nestled against her looking for milk. Whenever Paul or Ann expressed sorrow at the loss he would say, 'Tis only nature'.

I didn't want to dampen Ann's enthusiasm. If she and Paul were prepared to look after a tiny flock, I would approach the local lamb bank. I stressed it would be their job to care for them every day, no matter what the weather.

Just before Easter six tiny lambs settled down to a new life on a fenced off part of the rectory lawn. Initially they needed four feeds a day and the children took to their new task with great enthusiasm. The Heals helped with hay, and Paul learnt the skill of lighting a Tilley lamp which hissed as it provided light for the late evening feed.

Things went well for the first week, then one evening Ann came flying into the kitchen, tears pouring down her face. Out on the lawn four lambs were leaping and skipping about, but the two others were huddled together in a corner. We spread hay in one of the stables and carried the shivering creatures there hoping a warm place might help them to recover. Paul and Ann wouldn't leave them and pleaded with me to get Mr Heal to come round.

"They'm diers," he pronounced, shaking his head sadly. "They've given up poor things. Never mind, 'tis only nature."

Next morning Mr Heal removed the dead lambs and replaced them with what he called a 'good'n'. Paul and Ann were keen to give her a name.

"'Tis never aisy to give they names. If they 'as names, 'tis all the 'arder when they 'as to go."

The children couldn't quite grasp this and Ann persisted. "We could call her Dolly."

"Well, if you must, but 'ow 'bout callin' 'er Dorrie, like me missus. Us likes that name."

So that's what we called her. Dorrie turned out to be quite a character and being the greediest of our tiny flock quickly outgrew the four males. She was a terrible show-off and loved being the centre of attention.

The other lambs were given names too – Speedy, Pudding, James and Jumper.

Mr Heal's death came as a terrible shock to our family. He and his wife had been wonderful neighbours and Paul and Ann had taken to visiting them regularly.

Through her tears Mrs Heal sobbed, "We 'ave to be grateful. The arthritis was gettin' so bad, an' 'ed never 'ave coped with bein' 'ousebound. 'E 'ad such a strong faith, rector. No worries 'bout dyin', none at all."

Mrs Heal herself was crippled with arthritis and was now finding life lonely. She loved it when Paul and Ann visited. They chatted with her about the lambs, just as they'd done with Mr Heal, and told her all about poor James being ill; how they'd spent hours trying to feed him and just when they thought he was getting better found him dead under a tree. Mrs Heal listened sympathetically. "Now you two, remember what Mr 'eal used to say, 'tis only nature."

Mary and I had to be realistic. Three of the four surviving lambs were male and when big enough would have to be slaughtered.

"But what about Dorrie?" cried Ann.

With little grass, and no company during the winter months, it wouldn't be fair to keep her.

Now that her husband was dead, and their son wanted to reduce the size of his flock, the Heals no longer needed the extra land. The long-lost rectory paddock was ours once again, and with Jonathan Heal's help we set up our own small flock of nine ewes, including the much-loved Dorrie. Paul was overjoyed, as was Ann, especially now that Dorrie was safe. I, too, was happy to be returning to farming, albeit in a very small way.

Mrs Heal took a great interest in all of this. The children continued to visit her regularly, which she appreciated all the more since becoming housebound. Although not a regular churchgoer, from time to time she would ask me to give her Communion at the farm. I knew she prayed every night and loved reading her well-worn Bible.

In the last few months of her life she never complained. Her faith gave her an amazing ability to rise above the pain she undoubtedly suffered. Late one evening a phone call summoned me to her bedside. I prayed with her and sat with the family as she slipped away. Seconds before the end she rallied a little and a gentle smile spread across her face. "Us'll be goin' to Tom now. Us'll be goin' to join my Tom." I'm convinced she saw him at that very moment.

Next morning I met the undertaker at the farm and together with Jonathan we made all the necessary arrangements. Although Mr Oswald had come on business he seemed more of a family friend. Being a local man, if he was not actually related to his clients he knew most of them. We fixed the funeral for two-thirty the following Friday with refreshments in the parish hall afterwards.

That same day a Mrs Hayle died in a nursing home on the outskirts of Bristol. Some years before my time she and her husband had retired from London and bought a little house on the edge of Ashenridge. Mr Hayle died shortly after the move, and although Mrs Hayle wanted to remain in her own home, she found it hard living alone. She spent the next few years staying in turn with three nieces. Unfortunately, they could not cope with her increasing senility, and placed her in a nursing home where she spent the last years of her life. Visitors were few and far between.

While I was out Mary received a phone call from an undertaker by the name of Smith asking to speak to 'the reverend'. Nobody round here ever used Wild West language like that, least of all our local undertaker. He went on to tell Mary that everything was fixed for what sounded like Mrs Heal's funeral on Friday at two thirty and would she kindly tell 'the reverend' they only wanted a short service. What's more only one hymn would be sung – 'You'll never walk alone'.

Mary was completely taken aback by this extraordinary call. Why would a long-established family like the Heals choose what she could only describe as a spiv of an undertaker to handle their affairs. Surely arrangements had already been made with Mr Oswald. Perplexed, I rang the number Mary had jotted down.

"Good morning, reverend." Mary was right. The man's voice was smooth and slimy. Mr Smith assured me all was well, all cut and dried. When I replied that things were far from well or cut and dried his politeness evaporated and he made it clear he was not going to be messed about. "I'm sure you'll understand, reverend. It's too late now. We can't go upsetting the grieving families can we, reverend?" His voice sounded sickeningly pious.

It was obvious we must be talking about completely different funerals. I told him I had just come from the Heal family and Mr Oswald was their undertaker. They had already booked the church for two-thirty on the Friday for Mrs Dorothy Heal's funeral.

The silence at the other end of the line was deafening. When he eventually spoke it was to admit he was dealing with the late Mrs Hayle. He as good as said it was entirely Mary's fault, made it clear that nothing could be done to change the time, and rang off.

I was furious and immediately contacted Mr Oswald to warn him what was in the air. At the mention of the name Paul Smith he gave a short laugh – it transpired the two undertakers had crossed swords before.

Without any fuss, the Heal family said they were happy to change the time of their funeral to twelve-thirty with everyone gathering in the parish hall afterwards. Mrs Hayle's funeral would be at two-thirty followed by a gathering in the Coach and Horses.

Without my knowing it, Paul Smith had given the Hayle family my phone number and I now found myself having to finalise details with one of the nieces. She was most uncooperative, and objected to me asking any questions about the tribute being paid by a family friend. She was none too pleased when I asked for the title of the poem a child would be reading. The final straw came when I explained that 'You'll never walk alone' was a fine song, but not recognised as a hymn. She swore at me and insisted it was a family favourite. With that she broke down and I found myself talking to her husband, who was equally unhelpful.

Paul and Ann had become very attached to Mrs Heal, and we thought it only right to let them have a day off school to attend her funeral. My heart went out to Ann. She was very tearful at the start of the service and it was gratifying to see the loving way in which Paul comforted his sister.

As expected, the church was packed. The mourners listened carefully as I stressed that the church had been filled with flowers because the family wanted the funeral to be a bright and cheerful occasion, rather like Mrs Heal who always saw the best in everything. The singing was loud and lusty, especially for 'The Lord's my Shepherd', and the gathering in the hall afterwards was the sort of occasion Mrs Heal herself would have loved.

Mrs Hayle's funeral could hardly have been more different. Not one flower remained in the church. Her nieces regarded them totally unsuitable for such a sad occasion. Poor Mrs Pink. Even the fresh altar flowers she'd put in the church earlier that week had been discarded. Not knowing of their dislike of funeral flowers she'd good-naturedly reinstated them, only for someone from the Hayle family to throw them out again.

A small group had gathered at the church gate, all dressed in black, all smelling of alcohol, and all sobbing their hearts out.

As we entered the church they walked behind the coffin while the organist softly played 'You'll never walk alone'.

The mourners sat in the three front pews. Most of them wept loudly throughout the entire service. I often tell mourners not to be ashamed of crying, but this was different – after all Mrs Hayle had been shut away in a nursing home for several years and rarely visited by her family.

I read a short passage from the Bible. Then a little girl came forward and struggled to read a poem which included the words 'forever young in my memory'. It was hardly appropriate for a child who could rarely, if ever, have seen Mrs Hayle.

The tribute from a family friend was an utter disgrace. He'd obviously been drinking before the service and the only way he stayed upright was by leaning against the coffin. Once he got started I thought he'd never stop. His slurred speech produced an endless collection of anecdotes about the good old days when he and Mr Hayle were golfing partners. Mrs Hayle didn't get a mention! When he eventually staggered back to his seat someone yelled out 'good old Joe' and he was given a round of applause.

After 'Abide with me' – which only one or two of the mourners attempted to sing – I referred to the days when Mrs Hayle had lived in Ashenridge. This brought on another wave of crying.

Despite everything I wanted Mrs Hayle's family to go home comforted by my service. Such hopes were shattered when one of the nieces suddenly turned on me. Pointing to a mound in the cemetery she said accusingly, "Why couldn't you bury poor auntie in a lovely spot like this one? You've shoved her miles away. Nobody will visit her there."

I avoided getting into a heated discussion by explaining that Mrs Hayle had wanted to be buried alongside her husband. I'd hardly finished speaking when the undertaker came sauntering towards me. Mary was right about him. He'd come across as a spiv on the phone and he certainly looked like one with his slick black hair and veneer of politeness. He was clutching a bundle of banknotes and in front of everyone laboriously counted out a pile of one pound notes and crushed them in my hand. This money included payment for the organist, sexton and Church Council as well as my so-called fee. I could tell by their faces the family thought I was on to a good thing – all that money for half an hour's work!

One member of the Hayle family did take the trouble to thank me after the service. He asked if I ever felt depressed having to pass all those graves every time I went to church. Looking across the cemetery to Mrs Heal's grave I replied quietly, "No, not really. It's only nature."

Out of the corner of my eye I spotted a bewildered Mrs Pink retrieving her flowers yet again.

Chapter 9

Cakes and Guns

It sat on a big china plate on top of the old sideboard. A magnificent fruit cake that had Cedric's eyes almost popping out of his head. He could almost taste it. Surely Joe Rawlings hadn't baked it. And it was highly unlikely he would have bought such a large cake, unless he was expecting a lot of visitors.

At my request Cedric had reluctantly agreed to visit Joe on behalf of Westaleigh Church. Joe found it lonely living on his own, but when anybody visited him his face would light up and his eyes sparkle with delight.

"Come in, my flower," Joe would say. "Sit down and we'll have a chat." He had a fund of tales about the past. Anyone not knowing him might have supposed he'd spent his entire life on the farm, but Joe had actually lived in London for a while and he'd travelled over much of Western Europe during his time in the Second World War when he'd opted to join the army rather than remain at home in a reserved occupation.

The reason for Cedric's visit was to invite Joe, as an ex-serviceman, to lay a wreath on the war memorial at Westaleigh Remembrance Service.

Cedric hated anything to do with war, especially what he regarded as glorying in it. I told him that sooner or later he would have to overcome his prejudice because there would be no escaping it when he had his own parish.

As soon as Cedric mentioned the Remembrance Service Joe came out with a flood of memories. He delighted in recounting his experiences when liberating Italy, marching through France, and ultimately driving through a defeated Germany. "We had the Jerries on the run. Pop-pop-pop. We mowed 'em down, raced on scrambling over dead bodies, past burnt-out tanks, scorched corpses still inside."

Joe had got into his stride. "Out came the Jerries from their dug-outs, hundreds of 'em, hands in the air. 'Twas the end for them."

Cedric recoiled in horror. "Joe, you're talking about your fellow-men. Men with families. You must have felt like a murderer when you first killed a man."

"Didn't like it at first, but I wouldn't be sitting here now talking to you if I hadn't. It was they or us."

"But didn't you feel sorry, at least for the wives and children left behind?"

"There wasn't time to think about that. But you must know what I'm talking about, you've done National Service, haven't you?"

Without meaning to, Joe had touched on a tender subject. By extending his years of study, Cedric's call-up had been deferred and by the time his delayed papers came through National Service had ended. Cedric was no coward, but serving in the armed forces went completely against the grain. He saw all war as loathsome and could not tolerate those who gloried in it.

Having dealt with the war, Joe now moved on to another subject – the state of the nation. "You know Mr Palmer, I've no time for they mamby-pamby teachers. If the kids don't work they oughta thrash 'em. A good hiding never hurt anyone. And as for those goody-goody bishops who don't believe in hanging..."

This was all getting a bit too much for Cedric. He was already late for another appointment and still hadn't made arrangements for next Sunday. He needn't have worried. Joe felt honoured to be asked. "I'll be there, my flower. Don't you worry. But hang on a minute, can't you stay for a cuppa and a slice of cake?"

Cedric usually valued our time together at the Monday meeting, but today he kept fidgeting and couldn't wait to get away. "Cedric, what on earth's the matter? You're like a cat on a hot tin roof."

His younger brother was arriving that afternoon. "Why didn't you say? Bring him over for lunch tomorrow. Mary and I would love to meet him." Cedric hesitated then said he thought he'd better not.

That evening Mary rang Cedric to make sure he really meant what he'd said. A sharp voice answered: "Yes?"

Mary introduced herself and after some muffled sounds Cedric came to the phone. Mary felt sure he was about to say he wouldn't be accepting our invitation, but then a voice in the background said, "Why not? I don't care what they think."

Out of Cedric's car stepped a young man of about twenty, hair down to his shoulders. He could have come straight from the 'Long March' in China. He wore a Mao-type cap, a coat which buttoned up to the neck, jeans and sandals. A 'ban the bomb' badge was fastened to his coat.

So this was Cedric's younger brother, Steven. He told me with pride how he got himself expelled from a very exclusive school and then did the only thing real people should do – worked with his hands. In his case he'd helped build a magnificent block of flats for our heroic workers. Gone was the age of evil landlords exploiting the poor and housing them in terrible slums. He was proud to be a part of the new age of enlightenment where everyone was equal.

He looked at the rectory in disgust and mockingly suggested we turn our home into flats for more noble workers. Instead of preaching, I could devote my entire life to the welfare of the deserving residents. He certainly liked the sound of his own voice. Eventually we sat him down for lunch. Mary offered him roast beef. "No thank you." His voice was clipped and full of contempt. "Only animals eat animals."

When Mary brought in a trifle decorated with cream and cherries, he held forth about the iniquities of the leisured rich. He couldn't wait for the downfall of capitalism and went into raptures about the peoples of Russia and China living in the nearest thing to paradise on earth. Religion was the opium of the masses, the deadly poison, holding back the days of the glorious revolution. Funnily enough, he still managed to eat two helpings of trifle!

Cedric remained silent throughout all of this and Mary and I were relieved when Steven got into his brother's car. I would have been more impressed had this humble man opted to walk home rather than accept a lift in a capitalist's car. I couldn't resist a parting shot. "You know, I keep thinking about this earthly paradise of yours in East Berlin. It all seems a little selfish. Why do they hide it behind a wall? Why shoot the people who want to come out and tell the rest of the world about their wonderful lifestyle?" Cedric put his foot on the accelerator before Steven could reply.

Mary was so angry she didn't bother seeing them off. The noise of banging plates emanating from the kitchen said it all. "You know, Jack, I've never believed in corporal punishment, but I would love to have given that detestable young man a damned good smack."

The weather on Sunday the 10th November was so miserable that the party of ex-servicemen and the rest of the congregation sheltered in the church porch. They put off braving the wind and rain until just before eleven. The stranger sitting with them wore a Maoist outfit, and instead of a poppy in his lapel he sported a 'ban the bomb' badge.

Standing in the rain we remembered the names of the fallen, witnessed Joe placing the wreath on the memorial and observed the two minutes silence. We were all aware that the young man had remained in the porch, nonchalantly smoking a cigarette. Cedric looked decidedly uncomfortable. Although the pacifist in him may have identified with Steven's attitude, his pastoral heart must have been cringing.

Up until then Steven hadn't said a word, but as we walked passed him in the porch he waved something at us. "You can stick to your holy Bible – I'll put my faith in the Little Red

Book." He lit another cigarette and looked at us with an air of disdain.

This appalling behaviour rendered everyone speechless. Such was the mood of the congregation that I felt something had to be said before we attempted to pray or sing hymns. The words I used were totally unrehearsed and straight from the heart.

I climbed into the pulpit knowing I had to tackle the issue head on. I talked of the great cost so many had paid for our freedom and the fact that there were young people today who just could not see it. I spoke of my anger at what we had just witnessed. I described my dismay at the ignorance of a new generation who imagined themselves wiser than their fathers. Did they suppose we met on occasions like this to glory in war? Wasn't it ironic that young men like the one we'd just seen also gloried in bloody revolution? How tragic to see a child of this country disregarding the lives that had been lost so that we could enjoy freedom.

We were all subdued as we left the church and I lingered alone for a few moments by the war memorial. Beside the wreath of poppies someone had placed a simple bunch of wild flowers – was it foolish of me to think it could have been Steven?

Despite Cedric's efforts to keep it from the parish, people put two and two together and realised the young man was his brother.   He feared this would make his visit to Joe all the more difficult, but he felt a strong need to apologise for what had happened.

"Steven's not as bad as some people make out. It's unfortunate he's got in with a crowd of strongly opinionated students, but I'm sure he'll grow out of it. I'd no idea he was coming to the church on Sunday and I'm truly..."

Joe could see that Cedric was upset and felt sorry for him. "For all that's been said, you have to believe most of us don't glory in war. I remember as if 'twas yesterday the pathetic sight of the German prisoners, some little more than schoolboys. Like your brother, they were caught up by the fanatical fervour of youth and swept blindly into a mistaken cause. Look what it led to – war, defeat and bitter disillusionment." Joe sounded weary.

"Come on my flower, enough's been said. Us'll make a cup of tea." Cedric saw Joe's arm twitch as he reached for the kettle. Joe rolled up his shirt sleeve and revealed a horribly disfigured elbow.

"That happened in 1945. Our company had reached Berlin and we met with little opposition until we came across a sniper in a ruined building. The sniper didn't know a mother and her two daughters were hiding in that house. I discovered them and guarded them to make sure they didn't give the allies away. One of the girls had a beautiful face, beautiful fair hair. I don't know what made her move, but when I saw the sniper's gun I put my arm in front of her without thinking, to protect her. That's when I got shot in the elbow. Strange to think that after all that killing I saved the life of a German child."

Joe started pouring the tea. "Are you going to have a slice of this lovely cake or not? There's not much left and it'll be a while before I get another one." Joe laughed when he saw the puzzled look on Cedric's face.

"Now that's another story. Want to hear it?"

Cedric was going to whether he liked or not.

"A year or so ago a young woman came to my door. Her car had broken down. It was a terrible day, she was cold and I made her some tea. The fan belt had broken, so I did a temporary repair then sent her on her way to the nearest garage. She was so grateful she offered me money, but I couldn't take it. If we can't help each other without being paid 'tis a pretty poor world."

Cedric nodded in agreement.

"Anyroad, about six months after I came home to find a fruit cake on the draining board. No one round here knew anything about it, so I ate it. About six months later the same thing happened again. I still couldn't figure out where it had come from. Best fruit cake I ever tasted."

Joe poured Cedric another cup of tea and offered him another slice of fruit cake.

"Last week I'm out in the yard when this car drew up. I recognised her straight away. 'Twas the young woman I'd helped, you know the one whose car broke down, and there she was holding a fruit cake. The mystery was solved. Erna's job brings her this way a couple of times a year and the cake is her way of saying 'thank you'. We sat in the kitchen chatting over a cup of tea and it turns out she's German. You'd never have known it, her English was that good. Her family still live in Germany, and her father was a soldier in the war. He's coming to visit her next month and she'll be bringing him over to meet me."

Cedric wondered if there would ever be a right moment to relate all these stories to his brother.

"Well, the past's the past, and it's a good thing we're all friends now," said Joe firmly. "Come on, my flower, have another slice of fruit cake before you go."

Chapter 10

Short Skirts and Long Scissors

An eighteen-stone prizefighter barred my exit from the village shop. I'd only popped in for a bottle of milk, but Bessie Braun had no intention of letting me go until she'd had her say.

"Mr Longfield, it's b...y disgustin'. I've never heard such b...y foul language from those bell ringers of yours."

Her booming voice continued: "All I asked was for them to make a little less noise, and all I got back was a mouthful of filth. B...y churchmen, ringin' all times of the day and night. I wouldn't mind if they knew what they were doin', but it's the young ones and the terrible racket they make. I told them what I thought the other day. Can't repeat what they said. Worse language than a b...y public bar."

I looked around the shop hoping for a little support. Mrs Radd gave me a weak smile and for some reason found it necessary to rearrange a perfectly good display of tins on the counter. From behind the Post Office Mr Radd winked then carried on weighing and re-weighing the same parcel.

I tried to squeeze past, but Bessie had no intention of letting me go.

"Tell me, Mrs Braun, at what time do you normally wake on a Sunday?" She seemed taken aback by such a personal question. "Are you awake by ten thirty, the time the bells normally start ringing?"

Due to an influx of trainee bell ringers I knew there had been a bit of a racket from the tower on some practice nights, but bad language would never have been allowed by Bernard Chapman, the captain of the bell ringers. I assured Bessie that as their standard improved the noise would cease to be a problem, and I promised to have a word with Bernard. She seemed to accept this and grudgingly let me squeeze past, but the doorway was so narrow I couldn't move without my face becoming tightly squashed against her heaving breasts.

By the time I got back to the rectory I'd completely gone off the idea of a cooked breakfast. Mary wondered why I was looking so flustered and laughed when I told her what had happened.

"From what I've heard, poor old Bessie's been having a tough time of it. Her husband's always been a womaniser and rumour has it he's run off with Bernard Chapman's sister."

It so happened Mary and I were having family problems of our own. Ann had turned into a bit of a rebel and not a week went by without some sort of fuss or another.

"Your father will be furious when he gets home." Mary sounded upset and angry.

"I don't care. It's mine and I can do what I like with it," Ann screamed back at her mother.

As I entered the kitchen I could see the cause of the argument. Ann was wearing a short skirt, so short it barely covered her knickers. I recognised it as one we'd given her for her birthday, but instead of the hemline coming just above the knee she'd obviously cut it and it now ended just below her bottom.

"Dad, she doesn't understand."

"She, who's she? Do you mean your mother?"

Ann ignored me. "They tease me on the school bus for wearing a skirt down to my knees. All the other girls boast about their boy-friends and laugh at me because I don't have one."

She started sobbing, then giving me a defiant look cried, "But I have now and I'm not going to let him think I'm old-fashioned. We're living in the sixties, not the fifties. Dad, look around you, everyone's wearing mini-skirts. He's asked me out on Friday. It's his birthday and he's having a party at Leighford Football Club. I told him you'd take me there, but mum says I can't go." With that she flew upstairs to her bedroom and slammed the door.

Mary and I looked knowingly at each other. Ann had become a past master at throwing tantrums to get her own way. It was a pity she couldn't defend her own corner at school, but we were only too aware of the difficulties faced by the children of clergymen. It was a well-known fact their contemporaries tended to put them on some kind of holy pedestal.

Our son had had his fair share of teasing. One school friend insisted Paul must have been adopted because 'vicars don't do that sort of thing'. Paul treated such comments like water off a duck's back. It was different for Ann.

Mary and I were not always in agreement over Ann's behaviour, but Mary was right about the length of her skirts –

the school rules clearly stated they should come just above the knee. The other girls in Ann's class were either growing exceptionally fast or their parents were ignoring the rules.

I waited for a few minutes before going upstairs. 'She Loves You Yeah Yeah Yeah' was blaring out on the transistor radio, and Ann ignored me as I sat on the edge of her bed.

The loud music was giving me a headache and my patience was wearing thin, so I switched off the radio and hoped for the best. The silence in the bedroom was as deafening as The Beatles.

Thankfully, it worked, and Ann started pouring out her problems, the most serious being boy-friends, or lack of them. Eyes brimming with tears, she implored me to let her go to the party at Leightford Football Club, and I promised to speak to her mother.

She gave me a quick kiss on the cheek. "Thanks dad, thanks for being so understanding," she said innocently.

I'd hardly left the room when the transistor was switched back on at full volume. I walked downstairs to the music of 'It's Been a Hard Day's Night'. The Beatles were spot on!

Next morning Mary spoke to the mother of one of Ann's friends who said she would be helping with refreshments at the party. She reassured her that there would be adults present, and that the bar would not be open. This seemed to satisfy Mary and it was agreed I would take Ann to the party and collect her at a pre-arranged time. I warned her that if she put one foot out of place, or dared to criticise her mother, Friday's outing would be off.

What on earth was going on? The loud banging at the rectory door frightened the life out of me. An agitated Bernard Chapman was jumping up and down on the door step; behind him five junior bell ringers were hopping about, their ashen faces suggesting I had an emergency on my hands.

"You've got to come now, rector. It's that Bessie Braun. She's in the tower, she's gone stark raving mad, and she's goin' to kill someone with those scissors."

I could hear one bell with its stay broken ringing in an uncontrolled sort of way, but by the time we got to the church it had fallen silent. We climbed the spiral staircase to the ringing chamber and found it empty. The only sound came from one of the ropes which was swinging freely, as if an invisible hand was pulling at it.

Bernard kept looking around nervously. "Thank God, she's gone." He pulled a handkerchief from his pocket and wiped his brow.

"It was like this, rector." He told me how, during practice, they'd managed to raise all six bells at the same time. Their excitement at achieving this had been rudely interrupted when a furious Bessie Braun came storming into the tower brandishing a large pair of kitchen scissors and threatening to cut all the ropes. Pandemonium broke out and the bell ringers fled leaving ropes flying in all directions.

She'd made a wild lunge with the scissors at one of the ropes in an attempt to cut it, but it flew out of her hand and at the same moment another rope came down catching her under the arm and throwing her across the floor.

"Cor, didn' she swear," joined in one of the young ringers. Now they'd got over their fright they were eager to describe their terrifying experience. "She said we was all little b...s."

"She could 'ave killed us. Are you goin' to get the police, sir?"

Bernard continued: "After she'd picked herself up she started attacking another rope. She was in such a rage and made off down the stairs, still clutching the scissors and yelling she'd be back. She had a few choice words to say about you too rector."

As I approached her cottage the church clock was striking nine. A light was on in the front room and I could hear a radio or television playing loudly. Through a crack in the curtains I could see Bessie Braun asleep in a chair. How would she react if I woke her? Would she attack me with those scissors? Having knocked at the door, I now felt like running away.

The door was flung open and for the second time that week I found myself face to face with Bessie Braun's heaving bosom.

It wasn't easy having a conversation with someone who, only a short while before, had made such a vicious attack. My college training hadn't prepared me for anything like this. I took a quick look round the room and saw the scissors lying on the dining room table.

"Thank God you're here, rector. Thought you were the b...y police."

I could hardly hear what she was saying. Leaning as close to her as I dared I shouted at the top of my voice, "It's all right, I'm on my own." As soon as I'd said it I regretted not taking someone with me.

Bessie was far from being drunk, but there was a rip in her loose-fitting pullover, a bruise on her left cheek, and a plaster on the back of one hand.

"You've no idea what I've been through, rector. I've got to talk to somebody or I'll go b...y mad."

I still couldn't hear her and asked quietly, "What did you say?" This time she got the message and switched the television off.

Her story came pouring out.

"Probably before your time, rector, but my Frankie used to be a bell ringer. Good he was. Not the only b...y thing he was good at though, and not the only sort of bells he rang. I always knew he had an eye for the women, but I was head-over-heels in love with him and put up with it for years. Going off with Bernard Chapman's sister was the last straw. Our daughter left home because of her dad's rotten ways. Fancy leavin' home at seventeen. I don't even see Amy any more, but I know she's had a baby. What with her gone and now Frankie, I'm well and truly on me own."

No wonder she hated it when the bells rang. They were a constant reminder of Frankie Braun's bad ways, and she'd got it into her head that our captain, Bernard Chapman, was in cahoots with Frankie running off with his sister. Every time the bells rang it reminded her that Frankie had left her for another woman.

The next evening at tea-time I told Paul and Ann about Mrs Braun. They may have been regarded as sweet innocents at school but at home they often knew more about the realities of life than most children their age. They also understood that most things we discussed were confidential. I was hoping that Ann, being new to the world of boy-friends, would be warned by the story.

As promised, I took an excited Ann to the party in Leighford. I let her go in alone, but before driving off couldn't resist looking through the window. Everything seemed to be well organised. A buffet had been laid out on trestle tables and the music from the record player didn't seem that loud. I went home feeling relieved.

At about nine-thirty the phone rang. A distraught Ann wanted to come home. In the middle of the party her so-called boy-friend had abandoned her for someone else without even an apology. In between sobs she was saying something about all hell breaking loose when gatecrashers got into the bar and stole some alcohol.

I'll never forget that journey into Leighford. Mary came with me and by the time we got to the hall one or two other parents had arrived. Things seemed peaceful enough, but I could tell from the general mess and empty bottles that the party had got out of hand. Ann couldn't wait to get into the car and Mary sat in the back seat with her for the journey home.

We had a very distressing weekend with a heart-broken daughter, but by Sunday evening she'd pulled herself together.

"Thanks, dad, for telling me the story about Mrs Braun and her daughter. I don't want to make the same mistake."

She kissed Mary and me goodnight and said in a matter of fact voice, "But if I don't have a boy-friend it's going to be misery at school."

Bessie Braun found it punishment enough that the whole village knew what she'd been up to in the tower, and why. A much shamed Frankie Braun tried to worm his way back into her life, but she'd had enough and in full view of the neighbours yelled at him, "You're nothin' but a b...y bastard and you can sod off!" What Bessie wanted more than anything was to see her daughter and grandchild.

I didn't have much to go on, but thanks to the Mothers' Union network I discovered that Amy was living in a shelter for single mums in Whiteminster.

I had no idea what to expect when I called on Amy, and she didn't exactly welcome me with open arms. But then, why should she?

Three-month-old baby Peter was asleep in a cot. Amy made it clear that her plight was none of my business, but I couldn't leave without telling her a little of what had been happening at home.

"Fancy the whole parish knowing about the old hypocrite. It's about time everyone knew."

Once she'd started there was no stopping the stream of resentment she held against her father. Every time she'd done anything wrong, even the smallest thing, he gave her a long lecture on morality. When she got pregnant her father had said he would never allow her into his home with an illegitimate child – mum had been given no say in the matter. Amy knew all about his other women. Knew his whole life had been a sham. Then, turning on me, she cried, "You religious people are all the same. At least I'm honest and really care for my little boy. You go home and tell the village that and see how they like it. Yes, you can look at the scar father gave me when I found him in my bedroom trying to get into my bed. See the mark, there on my cheek?" She touched it. "He did that to me." Amy was shaking now and giant tears fell down her taut face. Realising she'd probably said too much she pleaded, "Please, don't tell mum, she never knew. No one ever knew."

After all my years of training I should have known what to say, but I couldn't find the right words. Instead, I put my arm around Amy's shoulder and gently rocked her. The tears slowly subsided and Amy looked lovingly at her son. "There now," she said softly. "At least I've got you."

Over the following months I visited Amy many times and she came to trust me. Clearly she could never live under the same roof as her father – she never wanted to set eyes on him again – but she and her mother were reunited and it was Bessie who found her daughter a tiny cottage to rent in Leighford.

A casual observer seeing the young woman carrying her baby into Ashenridge Church that afternoon might have thought little of it. But a very special occasion was about to take place. Amy and her mother had come to the church for the baptism of baby Peter.

A mixture of love and pride spread across Bessie's face as she watched her grandson being baptised.

"Peter Jack – I baptise you in the name of the Father and of the Son and of the Holy Spirit. Amen."

I was deeply touched that Amy had chosen 'Jack' as Peter's middle name. I was also touched by the change in Amy. The tight-lipped, wounded look had vanished and before me stood a confident, smiling young woman whose faith in human nature was slowly being restored.

Chapter 11

Nellie Mycock's Telephone

I couldn't believe my ears. Mary had casually informed me that social services wanted Nellie Mycock to have a telephone.

"No, not Nellie," I cried in disbelief. "If she gets a phone she'll be ringing morning, noon and night.

Mary tried to calm me down. "Jack, it wasn't my idea she should have a telephone. The social services are worried about her living on her own."

"Are they indeed, and are they going to be on the receiving end of her calls? No, it'll be you and me and the rest of the village."

Mary was not going to give way. "Jack, I promised you'd ring. They need your support because there's some sort of fund they can draw on to pay for the phone to be installed."

"They make it sound so easy, don't they, but you know who's going to pay the ultimate price. As far as I'm concerned, giving Nellie a phone is like giving your cousin Will a job behind the bar at the Coach and Horses.

To keep Mary happy I agreed to speak to the authorities, but not until the following day because I already had a number of calls to make in the parish and two in particular where I hadn't visited for a while. Walter Ringcombe was one of them.

"Can't think what I've done wrong, rector." He gave me a sideways look. "You've been round to all my neighbours, but you never come to see me."

This wasn't strictly true. I'd called on Walter several times in the last month but he was always out. Walter was passionate about his wine making and his elderberry and parsnip wines won him many trophies. Despite his sarcastic tone I could tell he was glad to see me. As we chatted he picked up a bottle from the sideboard and started filling two large tumblers full of wine.

"Did you know, rector, the elderberry's known as the Englishman's grape? Now tell me, what do you think of this one?"

To be polite I sipped the wine slowly.

"Come off it. That's no way to drink a Walter Ringcombe wine. You want to knock it back like this." With that Walter downed the whole glassful, and not wanting to offend I did the same.

"This one's even better. Comes from one of grandma's old recipes." Walter took my empty glass and filled it with parsnip wine.

"Best made in February, you know, and I wait a good six months or more before drinking it. Always get first prize at the flower show for this one. Good, eh?"

It was nearly three o'clock and I still had another call to make, but Walter was in full swing and wanted me to have another glass of elderberry wine.

"Walter, it's very kind of you," I said, putting the glass firmly back on the table. "Your wines are delicious, but I'm already late for my next call."

"Tell you what then, here's a bottle for you and Mrs Longfield. Reckon you'll both enjoy drinking that together. Bring the bottle back when you've finished and I'll give you a refill."

By now I was feeling quite mellow and wasn't at all surprised to see a cardboard box moving along the hallway. Walter was grinning from ear to ear. "She always goes in there when her time's nearly up."

He lifted a flap on the box and gently stroked the pregnant cat inside. "She'll be having her kittens soon."

Fred Gammin's cottage and back yard were permanently littered with oddments of old rope, branches, crates and boxes which he loved turning into rustic baskets, pots and garden ornaments.

He was a good neighbour to Walter Ringcombe and when he saw the bottle of elderberry wine began chuckling. "Been to see old Walter, have you? Surprised you're still standing! Come home from Walter's a bit the worse for wear myself sometimes. Mind you, whisky's my favourite tipple. Like to join me?"

"Not today thanks, Fred. Make it another time. I've still got half a day's work to do."

Fred took me through to the cobbled back yard. He loved showing off his latest creations. They had a charm of their own, and when he saw me showing interest in one particular pot he picked it up. "Now, rector, how about you take this for your garden. It'll look lovely planted up."

With the bottle of wine in one hand and a rustic pot in the other, I made my way back to the car. Smoke was billowing from Nellie's chimney. At first it smelt of burning wood, then I caught the sharp tang of burning rubber. She must be having a bit of a clear out. I crouched as low as I could to get past her cottage without being seen, and thought I'd got away with it when the gate swung open.

"What on earth are you doing down there, Mr Longfield?" Nellie noticed the bottle of elderberry wine. "No need to ask where you've been. Better come in for a few minutes, a cup of tea'll put you right."

As she fed the stove with bits of old packing cases, kitchen rubbish, chicken bones and the occasional piece of coke she never stopped talking. She eventually made a cup of tea then got down to the business of the phone.

"I expect you've heard I'm to have a telephone. Don't you think it's wonderful, rector. It'll make such a difference, and I've already started jotting down all the numbers. I promise you'll be the first on my list. Now what do you think about that?"

If only she knew.

Nellie was still talking nineteen to the dozen about the joys a telephone would bring when the clock struck five. I'd been with her for almost an hour.

Once Nellie's phone had been connected there was no stopping her. She rang the rectory morning, noon and night to talk about village affairs, the weather, something she'd heard on the radio or read in the newspaper. She rang one evening just as Mary was serving supper and kept me talking so long the meal was ruined. And we weren't the only ones. Nearly everyone in the parish was on the receiving end of Nellie's calls.

A few days later Walter Ringcombe waylaid me as I was driving past. "Got a moment, Mr Longfield? Come and take a look at this."

He was looking pretty pleased with himself and I soon discovered why. A proud mum and her five kittens were nestled in a basket in the corner of the kitchen.

"Beautiful, aren't they. I'm keeping the black one, and those three there are spoken for. I don't suppose you know anyone who'd like the tabby, do you?"

"Walter, you've given me an idea. Do you think a cat would help a talkative old lady who gets a bit lonely?"

"Good Lord, you don't mean Nellie do you? That woman's been driving me mad with her phone calls. Matter of fact, I got so cross with her the other day I told her a few home truths and told her not to ring again."

"Funnily enough I do mean Nellie."

"You're right. Pity though, 'cause I don't think she'll fancy having a cat from me, not after what I said to her. Tell you what though, she goes to Fred Gammin's every Wednesday for bits of wood for that old stove of hers."

Walter looked down at the kittens and grinned like a Cheshire cat. "You leave it to me rector, I've got an idea."

The following Wednesday Fred Gammin heard Annie's squeaky wheelbarrow and knew just what he had to do. As usual she began picking up old crates and boxes and couldn't believe her luck when she saw a particularly stout wooden box tucked away in the corner. Fred cried out, "No, Nellie, don't take that one."

"But it's lovely thick wood, just right for my fire," Nellie protested.

"No, better leave that one be."

Nellie was startled by a noise coming from inside the box. "Whatever have you got in there, Fred? What have you been up to?" she demanded. "Are you going to open it, or shall I?"

Fred opened the box and Nellie peered at the kitten sleeping inside.

"Last of the litter that one. Walter's found homes for all the others, but this little'n will probably have to be put down."

Fred looked so sad Nellie wasn't sure who she felt the more sorry for, him or the kitten. She looked inside the box again and gently lifted the purring kitten into her arms. "You tell Walter Ringcombe he should be ashamed of himself. I'll give her a home, and a good one at that."

As he watched Nellie pushing the wheelbarrow back home, the box and its precious contents balanced on top, Fred said to himself, 'That was easier than I thought'.

Nellie got such a shock when she opened her first telephone bill it rendered her speechless for the rest of the day. From then on her phone calls became few and far between and we all breathed a sigh of relief. But she still spent much of the day talking – to her constant companion, Tabitha.

106

It was Harvest Festival time and Nellie had asked me to collect some produce for the Sunday service. I could see her talking to Walter Ringcombe over the fence, Tabitha asleep in her arms.

As I got near I couldn't help overhearing what she said. "You know, Walter, our rector's a good man. But he should never have talked me into having that telephone."

Chapter 12

The Village Shop

If I hadn't been delayed by the school play, what an experience
I would have missed.

My visit to the three elderly Prince sisters was long overdue.
Martha was deaf, Betty suffered from a weak heart and Elsie,
the youngest of them, walked with a limp, the result of a riding
accident when she was only fourteen. Their parents had been
dairy farmers and the sale of the old farmhouse had provided
enough money for the sisters to live in modest comfort.

Badger Cottage was close to the main Leighford road. Half-
hidden by cypress trees, few people would have noticed it as
they went on their way to town. Away from the public gaze,
Martha, Betty and Elsie lived in a world of their own. The few
visitors they had were always made welcome, and I knew they
appreciated my occasional call.

A short track led to a small parking space. Heavily shaded by
overgrown trees and shrubs, it rarely saw direct sunlight and the
path was always muddy. Having been delayed at the school
play it was dusk by the time I reached the cottage and I was not
the only visitor. Mr Radd's delivery van was parked in the
drive. Betty opened the front door. "Oh, Mr Longfield, do

come in." She was struggling to catch her breath. "Only don't trip over the boxes." She put a hand to her chest and took a couple of deep breaths. "Mr Radd's here with our monthly supplies. You won't mind waiting a moment, will you?"

Climbing over the boxes I found myself transported back to another age. An Aladdin oil lamp lit the room and a large table resembled a market stall. In addition to running the Ashenridge village shop and Post Office, Mr Radd operated a delivery round. This evening he seemed to be displaying his entire stock – tins of all shapes and sizes, cakes and biscuits, fresh fruit and vegetables, flour, sugar, even soap and polish. Martha Prince was obviously in charge, but every so often her younger sisters shouted suggestions to her. Mr Radd stood patiently at one end of the table piling up all the things Martha had chosen.

I was fascinated and wondered how many other houses got this sort of treatment. In some ways I'd come at a bad moment, but I enjoyed witnessing this amazing ritual. When it was over we were invited to join the sisters for a cup of tea.

"Martha says you must have one of these chudleys," Elsie shouted, forgetting she was no longer talking to her deaf sister. She passed me a fresh cut round, generously spread with strawberry jam and cream.

Betty was busy going backwards and forwards to the huge black kettle steaming away over a crackling log fire. She constantly ran out of breath and struggled to fill the extra-large tea pot. She refused my offer of help, and the first cups of tea were as thick as the mud on my shoes – and almost the same colour.

While all this was going on, Elsie acted as interpreter to Martha.

"The rector wants to know how you are?" she shouted.

Martha beamed in my direction, from which I concluded she was well. Martha did not want to miss out on anything that was being said, and kept on shouting "What's he saying now? You know I can't hear." Everything had to be repeated several times and any attempt at anything other than the usual pleasantries was best avoided. This went on for some fifteen minutes and I was thinking it was time to go when Mr Radd dropped his bombshell.

"I'm not sure how much longer I'll be able to keep the shop going."

Betty and Elsie sat in stunned silence. It was a terrible shock for them. Mr Radd remained quiet for a moment while they took in the implications of what he was saying. The lamplight emphasised the deep furrows on his forehead and I could see life was beginning to take its toll on Mr Radd, and no wonder. He had a reputation for hard work and it wasn't unknown for him to make deliveries late at night. Indeed, it was a standing joke with some of the locals that he was their midnight grocer. I remembered a story that had gone round the village. One evening he was making late deliveries and a farmer's wife offered him a cup of tea. He sat down in an easy chair while waiting for it and promptly fell asleep. She left him in peace and came down the next morning to find him still there, a cup of stone-cold tea beside him.

Mr Radd went on to explain that his wife often felt unwell and was spending less and less time in the shop. With all the extra work he was finding it hard to cope, deliveries were getting later and later, and to cap it all they were making very little money. Nowadays village shops hardly paid for themselves – the ending of retail price maintenance had seen to that. Some goods were being sold cheaper at the supermarket in Leighford than he was paying for them at the wholesalers. Customers were being wooed by 'loss leaders', and most of the locals treated his shop as a convenience, only buying the odd thing they ran short of during the week. A business could hardly survive on that. The Post Office side helped, but it meant being open long hours and the pay was poor.

I couldn't imagine Ashenridge without a village shop and Post Office. Surely something could be done to save it?

You could bank on the village shop being quiet first thing in the morning. A pale-looking Mr Radd stood behind the counter; Mrs Radd was still in bed. I wanted him to know how disturbed I'd been by what he'd said the previous night. In view of all their problems I asked if Mary and I could help, perhaps give them a chance to have a rest. We wouldn't expect to be paid.

Mr Radd was completely taken aback and I could see he was going to reject my offer. "Don't give me an answer now. Think about it. Talk it over with your wife. We can only give short term help, but I dare say we could manage a week or two."

Over the next few weeks Mary and I made a point of going to the shop almost daily. No mention was made of my offer and we hoped everything was getting back to normal. That was until the For Sale sign went up.

"'Tis no more than they deserves," Len Cooksley commented. "You should see what they'm asking for sugar. 'Tis twice as much as in Fine Fare!"

"But do you know what they pay for it at their wholesalers? It'll be more than you pay over the counter in town."

"Well then, they'd best buy all their stock to Fine Fare."

"But, Len, Fine Fare is selling it as a loss leader to get people into their store. Once they get them through the door they know they'll sell them more, but not everything's a bargain. Some of the prices at Fine Fare are probably higher than the ones here."

Len, who always had an eye for a bargain, wouldn't listen. "If they'm offering 'lost leaders' at Fine Fare then that's where I'll be goin'. I 'ave to watch they pennies, I only 'as a pension."

I was sorely tempted to ask Len how he was going to collect his pension each week once the Post Office had closed!

Within a matter of days someone from Leighford had made an offer. We were thrilled by this good news until we learned the purchasers wanted to convert the premises into a private house.

This really made people sit up and think. Everyone knew about the Radds' problems, and when his wife was rushed into hospital Mr Radd rang me in desperation. He wanted to take me up on my offer, perhaps for a couple of days until they sorted things out. If Mary and I could keep the shop going he would continue with the deliveries. The Post Office was more of a problem because we would have to be sworn in and given instructions on how it worked. Mary and I had to go to the sub-office in Leighford and sign a declaration that we would not divulge any secrets concerning the Post Office.

Once people heard that Mary and I were temporarily in charge we had a steady stream of customers. Some were very concerned about losing the shop and promised to use it more regularly. When the Post Office was quiet I gave Mary a hand. Sweets, biscuits, cakes, tins of meat, dusters and polish, all went at an amazing rate.

Our busiest period came when the school bus stopped in Ashenridge on its journey from Leighford to distant farms and villages. For four or five minutes the shop was swarming with youngsters.

Some of the more colourful characters in the village who enjoyed expressing their opinions in the shop were embarrassed by my presence to begin with, but by the third day things were getting back to normal.

Old Charlie Swanson who came in for his baccy every day looked a bit coy when he saw who was serving him, but it didn't stop him telling a long-winded joke about a previous rector. His voice got louder and louder as he reached the climax. "So that was all 'e got for 'is whist prize – 'alf a pig's trotter. Har! Har! Har!"

It didn't take Peter Eastridge long to make an appearance. His look of triumph as Mary handed him his cigarettes said it all. As he left the shop he muttered, "Fine rector us's got." I had no doubt he would be in the Coach and Horses that evening declaring the parson was on the make again.

Those days I spent in the shop with Mary were some of the most valuable I'd ever spent in the parish. I got to meet people I would normally see only once or twice a year. Several came in with problems and unburdened themselves over the counter. The Radds had always leant a sympathetic ear and for some it came as a bonus that they could talk to the rector. Perhaps they found it easier talking there rather than in the formal atmosphere of the rectory. I was beginning to wish I could do it more often.

Friday evening was the day of reckoning when every stamp had to be accounted for, checked against the quota held on Monday, and balanced with the cash taken during the week.

While I was working on this with Mr Radd, the house agent turned up with the couple who planned to buy the property. They had no idea what the loss of the shop meant to our community and went round with a tape measure tactlessly talking about knocking down walls, removing fireplaces and replacing windows. Poor Mr Radd. As if he didn't have enough on his plate.

People kept asking me: "Why don't you do something about it?" But what? We were only helping for a few days.

One thing that did not clash with Post Office hours was Tuesday evening's Church Council Meeting. Mrs. Pink was annoyed that Mary would be missing that week's Mothers' Union meeting. I was ready for this. As far as the Mothers' Union was concerned, clergy come and go, and no church organisation should be totally dependent on the rector's wife attending.

I was also ready for them when they complained about my lack of weekly visits, and assured them that I'd spoken to as many people in five days in the shop as I would in months of visiting.

I tore into them with my main point. I spoke of the problems the people of the village might have in the future having to travel to Leighford for pensions and other essentials. As Christians we were supposed to show concern for our neighbours. Mary and I could help out for a few days in the shop, but what about others? I pressed the point again. Why not get a group of volunteers involved?

Annie Cook leapt to her feet and offered to organise a rota. She found no lack of offers and by the end of the evening nearly twenty people had put their names down.

Their efforts did not go unrewarded. A much happier and relieved Mr Radd took no time in letting everyone know that the doctors had diagnosed his wife was suffering from an acute iron deficiency which could certainly be put right. Shortly afterwards a large, handwritten poster appeared in the shop window which read: we send our heartfelt thanks to the people of Ashenridge for all their help and kindess. Mrs Radd is making a good recovery and thanks everyone for their gifts and good wishes. On the day the poster went up, the For Sale sign came down.

A few months later I called at Badger Cottage. A car which looked vaguely familiar was parked in the drive. Once again, a breathless Betty Prince opened the door. The Aladdin oil lamp was burning in the dining room, and a fine display of groceries had been laid out on the table. There was no sign of Mr Radd. Instead, Mrs Mathilda Pink was taking her turn on the evening delivery rota.

When the business was done, Mrs Pink and I were offered a cup of tea and a chudley. Martha Prince beamed away while Elsie relayed bits of our conversation at the top of her voice.

She smiled at each morsel of news, especially how the village shop and Post Office had been saved.

Elsie limped across to a cupboard and pulled out an elderly bottle of sweet sherry. It took her a while to remove the encrusted cork, and the dusty tumblers must have been sitting there for years. I got to my feet and raised my glass. "A toast to Mr & Mrs Radd *and* the village shop."

Martha looked flummoxed. "What did he say? They've got a new lad at the village shop?"

Chapter 13

Swedes and the Scented Lady

Something was up. The old ladies who met for their morning chat in the bus shelter were having a wonderful time. In fact they were so revelling in their piece of gossip they didn't even see me approaching. Had I been spotted, a sudden silence would have come over the assembly. Then, for my benefit, one of them would have come up with some polite comment about the weather. As it was, their flow of conversation continued unabated. I had no intention of eavesdropping and simply wanted to check that the poster for a forthcoming sale had been displayed behind the shelter. But I couldn't help overhearing their converstion.

"No! 'E never did that did 'e?"

"'Tis all true – every word of it."

"Tut, tut, my dear sowl," joined in a third, thoroughly enjoying the juicy bit of news. "If 'tis true, then 'tis nothing more than that one deserves. 'E bin askin' for it – plain greedy I calls 'n."

"But I tells you, us sawd 'n 'obblin' round next day."

"Cor, fancy that, but 'oo was it that did 'n?" asked another. "Does yer really think 'twas...?"

Talk about bad luck. The ten-fifteen bus pulled up at that precise moment and the name was lost to me. Who were they talking about? Some well-respected person who, in a moment of folly, had committed a terrible indiscretion? Or was it someone who had a reputation for sailing too close to the wind? I could think of half a dozen people that would fit.

Not wanting to appear nosy, I coughed diplomatically and asked if they'd read about the fund raising event advertised on the poster. We were working flat out to raise money for badly needed repairs to Ashenridge church roof and hoping for a really good turnout. I mentioned some quality items which had been promised for the jumble stall. I knew these would appeal to Kitty with her insatiable appetite for a good bargain. Kitty remained the uncrowned queen of the bus shelter. I'd come across her at this very spot when we first moved to Ashenridge, a cigarette hanging from her mouth, her smile disclosing a distinct lack of teeth, the few that remained badly in need of dental care.

There were several 'oohs' and 'aahs' when I mentioned that Lady Lavinia Woodhouse would be opening the event. She and her husband were well-known benefactors and we hoped their presence would draw in the crowds.

The ladies promised they would be turning up for the sale and would make sure everybody heard about it. As I wandered off to the village shop there were further whoops of delight as the ladies got back to their gossiping.

Fund raising events nearly always provoked a strong reaction from my curates. Roy Edwards had insisted they were a very unspiritual way of raising money and considered churches should be financed by straight donations and nothing else. Consequently, every time a sale was about to take place I had a tussle with him. Eventually even he had to admit that in the countryside such events are a valuable way of bringing people together. After all, nearly everyone living in a village, no matter how small their faith, has some interest in the church building, if only because one day they would be buried near to it.

Cedric Palmer had no problems whatsoever about raising money in this way, but he did object to bringing in some notable person to open the event. This went against all his socialist instincts. He may not have been a Maoist like his brother, but he had little time for the local gentry and hated seeing them given place of honour. I suggested he might prefer it if we asked a local scrounger to open the next one.

Ignoring my sarcasm, Cedric quickly changed the subject by asking if I had heard about the latest crime in the parish. Apparently someone had been caught in the middle of the night stealing swedes from Tom Hawkes's field. Whoever it was had been caught red handed and thrown the swedes back at their irate owner. Which was why Tom had been seen at Leighford market the next day, limping badly and with an ugly bruise on his face. Few people had any sympathy for him. Most felt he only got what he deserved.

"But who would want to steal swedes? I can't think of anyone round here who's that desperate. What I do know is this, Tom Hawkes is much better than people give him credit for." I told Cedric how I'd heard Tom's side of the story during the heavy snows of 1963. "He's not the extrovert and spendthrift his father was – that man nearly ruined the family business. It's taken years for his poor son to build up the business again. I deplore the idea that stealing from him is fair game. What's more, if I know Tom he'll be too much of a gentleman to say who attacked him."

Feeling exasperated, I left Cedric to decide whether or not he would come to the sale. If he felt he could not possibly taint himself by being present when a member of the landed gentry performed the opening ceremony, perhaps he should come later.

If fund raising events create tension between clergy, that's nothing compared to the effect they can have on the helpers. Nerves become taut like violin strings and the whole orchestra plays a symphony of complaints. On this occasion Mrs Mathilda Pink was annoyed because her stall was not in its usual place. Len Cooksley was upset because the jumble on the jumble stall was going to be a lot dearer, and he swore that 'raging inflation' had come to Ashenridge. To crown it all, the tea ladies were in a right dither because someone had commandeered their tables and they had to make use of some older ones.

Such music is part and parcel of parish life and something I'd learnt to live with, but the incident that was about to unfold was of a more serious nature. If the ladies in the bus shelter got hold of this one they really would have something to talk about.

Lady Lavinia Woodhouse cut a most striking figure. She wore a turquoise-blue suit and carried a handbag, made of the softest leather, which was nearly as large as her picture hat. The air around her was perfumed with the rich scent of lilies of the valley. She had an easy manner and mixed well with everyone.

Even Cedric, who'd forced himself to attend the opening ceremony, agreed she had great charm.

Before addressing the crowd outside the hall, Lady Lavinia asked if she might have a preview of the stalls so that she could find something fitting for her speech. I left her for a few minutes while she toured the empty room.

The apt words with which she opened the event were cheered to the echo. She concluded by holding aloft her huge handbag and said how she intended to fill it, just as she hoped everyone else would fill theirs. Having declared the sale open, she mingled with the crowd and was seen going round the room buying generously from each stall.

Most of the earlier troubles were now forgotten and I was thrilled to see the sale being so well supported.

Mrs Berridge had gone to great pains to make her bric-a-brac stall look attractive and I was hoping to find a present there for Mary. As I approached, she and her husband were having an anxious discussion and seemed oblivious to the long queue of people waiting to be served.

Seeing me in the queue, Mr Berridge pulled me aside and explained what was wrong. They were very upset because in an attempt to raise over £25 for the roof fund, he'd donated a delicate cut glass bowl which once belonged to his mother. It had an exquisite pattern of oak leaves etched on it and they were hoping to make at least £5 on this item alone. To their dismay it had disappeared, and Mrs Berridge had a horrible feeling it had been stolen. After all their hard work I was upset to see the Berridges looking so despondent.

This proved to be one of our best sales ever. Several stalls had completely sold out and, despite his misgivings, Len Cooksley had found not one, but three new jackets at a very fair price. Except for the unfortunate incident with the glass bowl everyone seemed happy, especially the treasurer who went home laden with bags full of money.

Mary and I strolled back to the rectory and looked forward to an evening in front of the television. We'd only been home a few minutes when the phone rang. It was Mr Berridge, still worrying about his missing glass bowl.

He sounded distraught. "We've racked our brains and feel sure it must have gone missing before the sale opened. We don't want to cause a fuss, but there was such a crowd...somebody could have slipped into the room without being noticed...or even hidden in the toilet at the back of the hall."

They were anxious to check the hall again. Reluctantly I went with them, cursing that I would now miss the one television programme I'd been looking forward to all week. As I'd expected, there was no sign of the bowl.

I'm no Sherlock Holmes, but the sequence of events the previous day had me pointing the finger of suspicion at one person and one person only.

I rarely make visits on a Sunday, but it was absolutely essential I call at Longridge Hall that afternoon. Fortunately I had a good excuse. Lady Lavinia had won a cake in the raffle but had already left by the time the draw took place. This was my opportunity to deliver it to her.

Still heavily scented with lilies of the valley, she ushered me into a magnificent drawing-room – an antique collector's paradise with displays of expensive porcelain, delicate glassware and beautifully carved ivories. She told me that almost everything had been passed down through her family and from time to time she enjoyed adding to her collection.

This reminded me of tales of Queen Mary who evidently had a habit of admiring other people's valuables in such a way that they felt obliged to give them to her. I steered the conversation round to the missing bowl and asked if she had any idea of its value. If Mr & Mrs Berridge decided to take things further with the insurers, or even the police, they might need to know how much it was worth.

If I'd touched on a tender spot, Lady Lavinia showed no sign of it, and it was only when we talked about the value of glassware that she gave herself away. I'd simply referred to a pattern of leaves on the missing glass bowl, but before she could stop herself she specifically mentioned oak leaves.

There was an uncomfortable silence and then she asked if we'd searched the hall thoroughly. I wanted to give her a way out of her predicament and told her that although we had searched the hall, I didn't think anyone had actually checked the glassware in the kitchen cupboard. Lady Lavinia suddenly remembered leaving her gloves in the hall cloakroom. As she would be going that way later on, would it be possible for her to get into the building?

I was more than happy to hand over my spare key, and concluded the case of the missing bowl was about to be solved.

A fair number turned out for the evening service, and there were smiles all round when I announced the treasurer had handed me £95, the proceeds of the sale.

"Our bowl would have made the total £100," Mr Berridge grumbled after the service. "Mind you, I'm not going to give up on finding it."

"Fair enough," I replied. "But one thing has occurred to me. I know we searched the hall from end to end, but did we look in the china cupboard?"

"I'm sure we did, but if you think it's worth it we'll take another look. No harm in trying."

I was not altogether surprised when a delighted but somewhat mystified Mr Berridge rang to say his wife had found the bowl. He added in a very suspicious tone, "Funny thing though, there was a strong smell of lilies in the hall."

When Cedric arrived for our Monday meeting he was in a foul mood. He'd taken a different route that morning and was annoyed when a sheepdog ran out from some cottages and chased his car. It had forced him off the road and his spotless car was splattered with mud.

I couldn't help chuckling. "Sounds like Mr Berridge's dog, Fly. Now that his master's retired Fly's taken to chasing cars instead of sheep."

The mention of Mr Berridge's name prompted Cedric to tell me the latest in the saga of the swedes.

In an effort to make his farm profitable, Tom Hawkes had diversified, planting swedes on some of the land formerly grazed by sheep. These fields were close to several cottages, one of which was owned by a retired farmer. Clearing swedes in late autumn can be a messy business, and for all his care Tom couldn't help creating some mud as his tractor went in and out of the fields. This led to a lot of strong feeling, especially from the retired farmer. Tom tried to be nice about it, and even delivered a bouquet of flowers to the man's wife, though his gift had been received with little grace. If only he'd thought more carefully about it, the odd swede or two might have been more welcome. As it was, the irate neighbour simply went and helped himself. That neighbour was none other than Mr Berridge.

Lady Lavinia was delighted to learn the missing bowl had been found. She very much hoped it might still be for sale, so I suggested she contact the Berridges.

Later that day I was driving past Tom Hawkes's field. He'd certainly made a good job of clearing the mud off the road. Mr Berridge was standing by his gate and waved frantically at me.

"Come inside, rector. We've got some good news for you. Lady Lavinia wants to buy our bowl – she's promised to pay £55 for it, far more than it's worth." He made it clear the full amount would be donated to the church fund.

"Funny thing is, when she came here she smelt of lilies of the valley. Just like the smell in the hall the night we found the bowl. Makes you think, doesn't it?"

"Certainly does," I replied. "But I mustn't keep you from your lunch. Those swedes smell delicious!"

Chapter 14

A Rose Between Two Monktons

It all began with an apparently harmless telephone call. "It's for you, Jack. The churchwarden from Dunkton is asking if you could take a Harvest Festival service for them?"

I was in the middle of discussing wedding plans with a young couple from the nearby parish of Combe Peter and quickly passed the diary to Mary, silently giving her the thumbs-up sign if the date was free. I had a particular fondness for Dunkton, having grown up on my father's farm near there. Although it meant a drive of some forty miles, I loved going back and meeting up with old friends.

"There's someone called Rose on the phone. She seems pretty het up. I think you'd better come and talk to her." This call followed hot on the heels of the earlier one.

"Now look here," demanded a high-pitched, autocratic voice. "How dare you push your nose into my affairs, wanting to hold a service without any authority from me."

For a moment I thought someone was playing a joke, but the voice persisted in a most unfriendly manner: "Rose of

Monkton. You know who I am, and I strongly object to you plotting behind my back with the churchwarden."

"Mr Rose, I think you must be mistaken. I don't even know your churchwarden."

"That's a downright lie." His high-pitched voice was trembling and resembled that of a soprano's. No wonder Mary had mistaken him for a woman.

"Can you deny that this very morning you and that fool of a churchwarden put your heads together and planned something behind my back?"

Mary had obviously made a mistake. The first caller had rung from North Monkton, not Dunkton. Furthermore, the person on the phone now was not a harmless old lady called Rose but the aged and quick-tempered Rector Rose of South and North Monkton.

I apologised profusely and promised I had no intention of interfering in his parish affairs.

The Windrush is a modest river which, over the centuries, has carved for itself a deep and beautiful wooded valley. It rises on the windswept moors beyond North Monkton and descends rapidly into the lush green valley below, swelling as other tributaries join it. By the time it flows under the ancient stone bridge at South Monkton, the Windrush is a respectable river in its own right. Its journey continues on past Westaleigh until it joins the River Badger at Leighford. Brown trout and the occasional salmon can be found in its deep pools.

At South Monkton this river once provided power for the corn mills, but that was but a distant memory. Over the years the mills and many of the surrounding cottages had been converted and snapped up by the wealthy. Only a few cottages remained in local hands. To keep abreast of the times, incomers took it upon themselves to give the long-established Mill Inn a more appropriate name, and it was now known as The Angler's Rest!

The beautiful church of South Monkton stood in the centre of the village. Built in the fourteenth century, it was renowned for its stunning stained-glass windows and mediaeval carvings. Rector Rose lived alongside the church in an elegant Georgian rectory, its extensive grounds sweeping down to the River Windrush. On the other side of the church, high iron gates led to Monkton Court, home to Squire Rose, and for many generations home to the Rose family.

Like many of his predecessors, the present rector was closely related to the Roses at the big house. This family was patron of the living, meaning it was responsible for selecting clergy to serve here. Hitherto they had had no difficulty in providing a candidate from their own family, but Sebastian Rose was the last of the line. Now approaching eighty, the archdeacon had decided that when Sebastian retired the Monktons could no longer warrant having their own rector. Rumour had it they would join our Badger Group of parishes.

The people of South Monkton hated this idea, and poor Sebastian Rose could think of nothing worse than his parishes suffering such an awful fate.

There could hardly have been a greater contrast between the villages of South and North Monkton. The latter was not really a village at all, just a collection of farms and occasional cottages ranging over miles and miles of upland countryside. Years ago the people who lived there would have been tenants of the South Monkton Estate, but the properties had been sold between the two wars to cover death duties.

North Monkton's original church had fallen into such a bad state of repair that by the 1840s it had to be razed to the ground. Thanks to a philanthropic member of the Rose family, a new church was built in exactly the same spot as the first one. Sadly, it was far too large and had a high-pitched roof that was impossible to maintain.

Sebastian Rose hated the building with a vengeance and could never understand why a band of six faithful worshippers persisted in turning up there every Sunday. He unkindly named them his 'indestructibles'.

Against all odds, the people of North Monkton parish were determined to remain independent. Although the school had been forced to close in the 1930s, the parish had managed to retain the building and converted it into a hall where whist drives, socials and Christmas parties were held.

Mr Rose became a past master at avoiding services in North Monkton and tried, in vain, to persuade the congregation to come to South Monkton. He craftily reduced the number of services each year from fifty-two to twenty-five, but nothing could kill off his 'indestructibles'.

It seemed as though God had thrown his full weight behind Sebastian Rose. Frost lifted the old rendering, violent rainstorms saturated the weak cement, and gales tossed slates from the roof like confetti. Not one brave person could be found to repair the high-pitched roof at North Monkton. The archdeacon and his surveyor were asked to carry out an inspection, and Sebastian knew his prayers had been answered when the church was declared unsafe. He lost no time in personally affixing 'closed' notices to every side of the building. But if Sebastian thought he'd won the battle he was wrong. The people of North Monkton resented the attitude of the religious hierarchy and dug their heels in.

Which was why their churchwarden, James Smallcott, had taken matters into his own hands and invited me to take a service at North Monkton.

The archdeacon held a meeting with the North Monkton Church Council to discuss the permanent closure of the building. He took up Mr Rose's cause but, naturally enough, met with fierce opposition.

He could not understand why these diehards refused to give up their own church and worship at South Monkton. It was only a few miles away. Did they not realise how much money would be saved by having only one church to maintain? Could they not see that a congregation of twelve in the lovely church at South Monkton was far better than a congregation of six in a crumbling ruin?

The parishioners were happy in the knowledge that the diocese could not close North Monkton without their consent. But Sebastian would still not give up and applied further pressure by telling the parishioners not to have their relatives buried there because 'one day the churchyard will disappear'. Thankfully, his words fell on deaf ears.

In the fullness of time it was likely that James Smallcott would act as one of my own churchwardens, and although he'd broken the rules of etiquette by going behind Sebastian's back, it was important I keep things on an even keel with him. We sat in my study discussing the future of North Monkton, and I half-heartedly tried to take the opposite point of view, not because I believed in it but to show loyalty to Sebastian Rose.

I asked Mr Smallcott why the parishioners felt they could not worship with their neighbour. He explained that long before the present campaign there had indeed been a well-established tradition of the North Monkton parishioners attending major services at South Monkton. But as time went by it became obvious that north was always expected to go south – south would never contemplate going north.

I then suggested that if they disliked the idea of pairing with South Monkton, why not try linking with another nearby parish. Mr Smallcott retorted by asking how I would feel if I and my family were expected to spend all our time with neighbours instead of enjoying our own home? A fair point, but how could he be so sure there was such a strong family feeling in so scattered a parish? I was surprised to learn that out of a population of only two hundred plus, at least seventy-five came to the socials, even more to the Christmas party.

Why then, if the church was so important, did only six come to worship – a figure that hardly suggested a whole community pulling together? Were they not being selfish holding on to a large, run-down building and expecting the diocese to provide ministry for them? If the congregation was so small, surely it could travel elsewhere? This solution had been tried and proved in other parishes.

Mr Smallcott frowned for a moment, fearing his potential rector might be no better than the present one. His reply amazed me. He started by quoting success stories of other churches in similar scattered parishes with no village centre. He admitted Mr Rose was reasonably good about visiting the sick and bereaved, but at the same time he upset people by talking about closing the churchyard. North Monkton was their home and they wished to be buried with their forbears. Furthermore, on the rare occasions Mr Rose came to North Monkton Church, he deliberately led a dull, short service and did nothing to draw in a younger generation of worshippers. With the closing of the church a kind of spiritual emptiness had descended on the community. Without the church at its centre, the parish of North Monkton was losing its soul.

What was I to do? I sympathised with Mr Smallcott but made it clear I could not go behind Mr Rose's back. It was a complex situation.

Within days of Sebastian Rose suffering a stroke, the Bishop of Whiteminster contacted me saying he would like the parishes of South and North Monkton to come under my care. As expected, this met with fierce resistance, headed by Squire Rose of Monkton Court. As patron he had a say in any new appointment.

The archdeacon visited the parish and warned him that the ancient endowments could only produce £400 annually towards the stipend of a new rector. Unless the people could come up with at least double that amount they could never afford to have their own rector. If, however, they joined with my four other parishes that would make all the difference. Squire Rose was given six months to sort things out. When he failed, the bishop put a proposal to him. As the diocese had no immediate use for the rectory, Sebastian could continue living there.

This helped to sweeten things a little and, there being no alternative, the parishes of South and North Monkton passed into my care.

It's not always easy for a new rector if the previous incumbent is still living in the parish. It's even more difficult if that person is a strong-minded reactionary. I could have simply ignored Sebastian, but that was not my way. Even if we disagreed, he was still a man of God who had given most of his life to serving the two parishes, and undoubtedly had done much good work.

It was such a pity he found himself at odds with me and the diocese. As of now he was one of my parishioners and I felt it only right I should do my best to befriend him.

The door was opened by Sebastian's housekeeper. Without a word passing between us, she led me along a dark passage lined with paintings of hunting scenes, then through to the heavily furnished drawing-room where ancestral portraits hung on dull green walls.

Sebastian lay on a *chaise-long*, propped up by a mountain of pillows. So this was the quick-tempered Rector Rose – hardly the man who'd lambasted me on the telephone. The stroke had left him with a twisted, half-open mouth and each time he spoke he dribbled.

"Come nearer to me. They say you are the new rector. I had cross words with you once…now you have got what you want…I cannot agree with your new ideas, but I don't wish you ill. In time you will learn I was right."

The strain was showing in his face. There were tears in his eyes and his voice was getting weak. "Thank you for calling, Mr Longfield. I must rest now. I wish you good morning."

Brief though the interview had been, it was still very moving. Sebastian had spoken with sadness rather than anger, knowing that all he'd achieved during his long ministry was coming to an end. The future lay in the hands of someone he feared would destroy much of what he'd accomplished. It wasn't going to be easy, but I was determined to prove him wrong.

Cedric loved the mediaeval carvings and paintings in South Monkton Church and begged me to let him visit there to take some of the services. I agreed on condition he also worked in North Monkton. I warned him he would be exposed to a lot of ill feeling, mostly stirred up by the Rose family and their friends, who I suspected would try to play us off against each other.

The warm-hearted people of North Monkton were no problem. I felt sad that Sebastian had failed to appreciate them. I could see why they valued their community so much, even though it was not going to be easy to provide the regular services they wanted. Unlike the archdeacon, the Bishop of Whiteminster was delighted at the prospect of North Monkton Church coming to life again. Indeed, he supported my idea of using local churchwardens and other lay people to take short services there.

With the closure of the church, and because the hall was far too large, Mr & Mrs Smallcott kindly offered the use of their sitting room as a temporary measure. I made a point of attending a couple of these services and took to the people instantly. I wished I could spend more time with them, but with six parishes in my care I never had a spare moment.

Over the following months the half-dozen communicants grew until they totalled a dozen. This, however, was nothing compared to the family services. The parish was fortunate in that several young families lived in and around the area and Mrs Smallcott also started a Sunday School.

Housing everyone in their sitting room soon became an impossibility. That Christmas, when the families and the 'indestructibles' all met together, they ran out of space and the congregation spilled into the rest of the house. Some found themselves sitting half-way up the staircase!

The next year we moved into the hall for services, but with numbers still growing it became obvious the church would have to be restored and adapted to modern times.

Hearing about our plight, a local architect drew up plans for a very modest fee. These included lowering the ceiling and partitioning off a space at the back of the church to house the vestry and Sunday School.

By sheer hard work, and some modest grants, the parish raised the £3,000 needed for the work, and to ease costs a handful of parishioners gave up their free time to work alongside the builders.

Squire Rose and Sebastian Rose would not climb down off their pedestals and opposed the re-building in every way they knew how – and claimed to be speaking on behalf of the parish. Apart from their employees, nobody agreed with them.

After months of hard work, North Monkton Church was ready, and the Bishop of Whiteminster accepted our invitation to attend the opening ceremony. Invitations were sent to Squire Rose and Sebastian Rose – they both declined. Although Sebastian was making something of a recovery he felt it would be unwise to make the journey.

Of all the others invited there was one noticeable absentee, the archdeacon, who declared he could see no point in rescuing a 'twopenny halfpenny' church from oblivion. I'd disliked him from the start – I disliked him even more now.

In one way or another almost every parishioner had been involved in the fund raising. Others had spent hours cleaning the church and sugar-soaping, staining and polishing the discoloured woodwork and pews. Not one of them missed the service.

Without the bishop's support and encouragement, I knew we could never have taken on such a massive undertaking. He had true vision for the future of the country church. There must have been times when he found himself standing alone over such issues. Behind the scenes he probably had many a tussle with urban-minded diocesan officials who simply wrote off places like North Monkton.

On this occasion it was obvious it gave him the greatest of pleasure to join in our celebrations and re-consecrate the building. Rather than simply reviving the past, he confirmed that this church, with its simple, home-run family services, really was looking to the future. A day might come when there would be fewer clergy and churches like North Monkton would have to stand on their own two feet, but he rejoiced in the fact that by restoring the church we had 'put the heart back into the community'.

Needlesss to say, the church was not packed every Sunday. The regular congregation was drawn from a nucleus of about twenty adults with many more coming for special occasions. And then there were the Sunday School children. Not only did they come to the family services, but some of the older children had formed a small choir.

Not long after the re-opening, a working party met to have a major blitz on the untidy churchyard which, inevitably, had been neglected during the building work. Beneath a jungle of brambles they discovered a stone commemorating the consecration of the new church at North Monkton – it was dated the 20th June 1846 and bore the name of the then rector of the parish, Reverend William Rose.

It seemed only right to reinstate the stone in a prominent place, and the wall by the entrance porch was deemed the most appropriate.

It also seemed right to invite both Squire Rose and Sebastian to the dedication. Squire Rose, who infuriatingly referred to North Monkton Church as his great-great uncle's 'folly', declined, as did Sebastian.

On the morning of the dedication Mary called me into the study. "It's Sebastian Rose. Wants to talk to you about this afternoon."

I thought perhaps he was going to offer his congratulations or wish us good luck. His high-pitched voice was instantly recognisable and sounded less shaky than the last time we'd spoken. "Thought I should let you know I'll be coming to the dedication after all. Don't want any fuss, I'll only be staying a few minutes."

His words were a joy to my ears. After all our trials and tribulations perhaps things were at last moving in the right direction.

We invited the rural dean to dedicate the stone, but on seeing Sebastian arrive he graciously invited him to perform the ceremony. Everyone waited with baited breath as the old man hesitated before nodding his head in agreement.

Sebastian's housekeeper wheeled him as closely as she could to the entrance porch. Brushing her aside he struggled out of his wheelchair and stood firmly on his feet. With the help of the rural dean he read the appropriate words and drew back the make-shift curtain to reveal the stone.

There were tears in his eyes as he stood gazing at the inscription. He thanked everyone for their remarkable achievement then, with the help of his housekeeper, sat back in the wheelchair.

His handshake was strong and had real warmth to it. He didn't say another word – he didn't need to.

Chapter 15

Troubled Times

"Mr Longfield, Mr Longfield." The anxious voice of Annie Cook was calling me from the other side of her hedge. "Can you spare me a moment?"

A summons like that usually meant another list of people who needed a visit from me. At her best Annie could be a very helpful friend, at worst a rather trying busybody whose one mission in life was to ensure I was always kept fully occupied. She was like a walking conscience watching me every time I went into the village.

I told her I had enough on my plate that day and couldn't face another list. She ignored me and insisted, "I really think you ought to know what people are saying."

My heart sank. What had she got hold of this time?

"Mind you, I don't think it can be true. I'm sure there's some explanation. You know what people are like. Only you do like to know what's being said."

"Out with it then, Annie. Who's been up to what?"

"Well, it's about one of your churchwardens," she said, taking off her gardening gloves and pointing in the direction of

Combe Peter. Then, looking round to make sure nobody could hear whispered, "It's the Birchalls. You know, at Combe Peter."

Well, of course I knew the Birchalls, but having six parishes to minister I didn't see them as often as I'd have liked. Combe Peter was the smallest of my six parishes and Steve, the churchwarden, and his wife, Rita, had worked wonders there.

"A rumour's going round they've split up. Nobody knows where she is, and he's got some fancy woman living with him. I know that's true because I've seen them go by in the car. It's not his wife with him – this woman's got fair hair. There now, but I expect there's nothing in it. We all know how people talk."

I could not believe it. The Birchalls were a devoted couple, and devoted to their work at Combe Peter Church. Thanks to their enthusiasm a once-dwindling congregation of six had mushroomed and over the last few years people of all ages had been attending, especially the family services for which they'd worked so hard.

It was true that things had not gone so well just lately. The young children who'd first started coming to the church had reached their teens. Some were preparing for Confirmation whilst others had quietly faded away. In small communities families often come and go in waves. For years there seem to be children everywhere, then they grow up and there can be quite a gap before another generation appears. I knew Steve and Rita had been worried by falling numbers, but I'd reassured them that children brought up in the faith often returned as they grew older.

Rapid success at Combe Peter had generated a problem no one could have foreseen. Instead of becoming more outward looking, the congregation became 'house proud'. Having installed electric lighting and purchased new hymn and prayer books, kneelers, communion cloths and altar frontals, the parishioners were forever thinking of more ways to improve their own church and were totally oblivious to the needs of others. 'Missionaries' was a dirty word, and charity something to be resisted. There was always a fuss over paying dues to the diocese, and no matter how hard I tried I could not convince the people of Combe Peter that their contributions to central funds helped maintain their ministry.

At the last meeting the Birchalls overturned all this. I don't know how they did it but Rita, as secretary, read out a letter of appeal from the Children's Society which would normally have been politely dismissed.

Rita proposed that a representative be invited to speak at a Sunday service at which the proceeds of the collection would be donated to the Children's Society. Also, she asked everyone to support a coffee morning with the proceeds again going to the society. For once the Combe Peter Church Council did not come up with their usual objections.

Why would the Birchalls want to venture into such a project if they were on the point of separating? There was only one way to find out. This dreadful rumour must have been started by someone who resented the decision to support the Children's Society.

Combe Peter Church Council was due to meet that very evening and I would make it my business to be there.

I was looking forward to the meeting and felt sure that any rumours about Steve and Rita would evaporate when people saw them together. Unfortunately I was wrong.

Rita wasn't even there. A surprisingly subdued Steve kept very much to himself before the proceedings began, and then mumbled some sort of apology about Rita being away. He read out her minutes in a monotone, stumbling from time to time over the writing. My heart sank. Could the rumours be true?

When the minutes about the Children's Society were read, Mrs Small reminded us that we were planning to replace the harmonium with a pipe organ which would take up every penny we earned. Steve said nothing, and despite my protests about going against the decision made at the last meeting, the pipe organ won the day.

The special service and coffee morning had already been announced in the parish magazine and I hoped this might shame them into changing their minds. It did not. As soon as the meeting was over, Steve shot away without giving me a chance to speak to him. I returned home feeling deeply disturbed.

I had to burst the bubble, so I drove over to Combe Peter the following day on the pretext of needing Steve to sign some important documents. He must have missed seeing my car as it made its way down the hill towards the small lay-by where his visitors normally parked. A thick fir hedge hid any callers until they reached the top of a flight of steps to the house. I came in full view of the large sun lounge at the front of their bungalow and to my dismay saw two figures embracing. When they spotted me they separated. I only got a glimpse of the woman. As Annie had said, she definitely had fair hair.

Stephen seemed miles away as he opened the front door. Normally he would have invited me in, but today he stood indecisively in the doorway.

I offered to leave the documents and return the next day to collect them.

"No need," he said absentmindedly. "I'll sign them now."

He took a pen out of his pocket and without giving the forms a second look signed them and hurriedly passed them back to me. I apologised for being a nuisance and started to ask after Rita. Steve was already closing the door and I was left standing on the doorstep.

Everything seemed to confirm my fears, especially when Steve did not appear in church the following Sunday. He sent no word of apology. Mr Hammond, the other churchwarden, had also heard the rumours, but like me had no way of knowing whether or not they were true. After the service the congregation seemed in a hurry to get home rather than stay and chat – most unusual for Combe Peter. Something had to be done, but what?

Unfortunately troubles never come singly. The headmaster had rung Mary to inform her that Ann had been caught truanting when she should have been in school. This was sad because Ann was a clever girl, but I knew she was still finding it difficult to cope with the relentless taunts about being a clergyman's daughter.

That night I talked it over with her and tried a different approach. I asked her about the children who were respected at her school. She thought for a moment and then listed them – girls with good looks; sporting stars; strong-minded extroverts. One of these 'stars' was the daughter of a Methodist minister.

"I've just remembered. Sally's in the cross-country team. Dad, what about running, do you think I'd be any good at it?"

Leighford Grammar had a good reputation for sport and particularly cross-country running. At first Ann hated it, until one day she got second breath and said she could have gone on running forever. A race was coming up and she was determined to get into the team. It was good to see our daughter using every spare moment to practise along the country lanes.

Steve Birchall rang and, without giving anything away, asked if I would go round and see him.

My heart was in my mouth as I approached the house. Although they weren't actually embracing, the fair-haired woman was in the sun lounge again and Steve was with her. How dare they be so brazen. How dare they flaunt themselves like this and in such a small parish. What on earth was this doing to Rita, who probably knew that the 'other woman' was in her home, perhaps even in her bed? I prepared myself for the worst, to hear a story about a broken marriage.

A very distressed Steve opened the door. He showed me into the sun lounge and introduced me to Janice Mitchell, his sister. With immense relief I sank into the nearest chair, but my relief was short lived.

Janice took both of her brother's hands in hers and pleaded with him to talk about Rita. "You can't keep it locked inside any longer, Steve. You must talk about it. You can't change what's happened. You're going to make yourself ill." Her voice tailed off and she started to cry. "I'm sorry, Mr Longfield." Janice ran from the room and I turned to Steve. "For God's sake, tell me what's happened."

Steve started talking, his voice weary and lifeless. "I'm going to lose her, Jack. I'm going to lose the most important person in my life, and I can't do a thing about it." Slowly he gave me the dreadful news. Rita was in hospital. She had cancer. When she first discovered the lump in her breast she kept quiet about it for almost nine months. By then it was too late, the lump was diagnosed as 'aggressive' and the cancer spread like wildfire throughout her body.

"If only she'd gone to the doctor. She didn't even tell me about it. There's no hope. My darling Rita's going to die."

I spent much time that Sunday silently praying for Rita and Steve. Mary found it hard to accept that the cancer could take a hold so quickly. Both Paul and Ann said they would pray for a miracle, because miracles do happen. None of us felt like supper and we went to bed with heavy hearts.

The change in Rita was so dramatic I thought I must be in the wrong room. Her lifeless eyes gazed up at me and it was a while before she recognised me. "Jack, you've come. I was hoping you would." Her voice was so weak I could hardly hear what she was saying. I sat with her and we held hands. I sensed something was troubling her. "Are you in pain, Rita? Shall I call the nurse?"

Rita shook her head. "I needed to talk to you. I needed to tell you how I failed everyone. When I was young...I had such great plans...especially after joining my church...I wanted to put the world right...I planned to be a missionary...then I wanted to have a...to have a family."

Her sunken eyes filled with tears and we sat in silence for several minutes.

When she spoke again it was to repeat her sense of failure. She came from a very committed church family who held out great hopes for her. As she grew into her teens, she realised she could never be the Florence Nightingale or Elizabeth Fry her parents had hoped for, so she reacted and for a while rebelled against her religious upbringing. She kept saying how guilty she now felt about the anxiety she'd caused her parents at the time.

She met Steve who, at the time, had little interest in the faith. To please her parents they decided to marry in church, and it was during the marriage preparation classes that her faith was restored. She joined in the life of a very lively suburban church, and step-by-step Steve came to appreciate her faith. At last she was getting a vision of what God wanted her to do with the rest of her life, but she became very frustrated when Steve told her she had to be realistic. Yet another chance came when Steve decided to give up his business and Rita dreamed of taking Bibles to China, learning the language and spending time out there encouraging oppressed Christians. Instead she found herself growing fruit in sleepy Combe Peter with its then very dead church.

I reminded her that it was thanks largely to her faith and determination that the church here had come to life. It had grown in numbers and enthusiasm. She insisted this was all Steve's work.

"No Rita, you did it together. Steve couldn't have done it alone, he did it with you by his side."

Her face lit up momentarily, but I could see she needed to sleep. We prayed together for a short while and I promised to return the following day.

The nurse warned me that Rita was extremely weak and it would probably be best if I only stayed for a short while. I thought she was sleeping and sat quietly by her bed, holding her cold hand in mine.

Who can say where her strength came from. She suddenly grasped my hand with such remarkable force it made me wince. At the same time she stroked her stomach with her other hand.

"We were so happy when I got pregnant. We'd tried for ages and it seemed our prayers had been answered." Rita's eyes filled with tears. "The baby was stillborn, and the doctors told me I could never have another child. Steve was wonderful. He took such good care of me, but deep down I felt my life was pointless. Children have always been important to me." Rita's voice was growing weaker and I thought she might need the nurse.

"No, I must finish Jack. I had to accept what had happened. If I couldn't have a child of my own then at least I could do something for others. That's why the Children's Society has been so important. But I've never been able to lose that sense of failure. Why?"

"Perhaps it wasn't so much a sense of failure. It seems to me you were always striving to help others. You may not see it, but the parish knows how tirelessly you've given of your time to make Combe Peter what it is today. You and Steve together. Be glad, Rita, that you are responsible for the young ones who come regularly to the family services. Some of them will go on to be confirmed, and you know that one is seriously thinking of becoming a missionary.

"Without you, Rita, none of this would have happened. Please believe me when I say you will live on in the lives of so many of the youngsters who come to your church."

A few days later I held a bedside service for Rita and Steve. There was an air of calm about her and for someone so ill her voice was unbelievably strong. Gone were the anxious lines on her face as she looked with pleasure at the flowers from her many friends and at the beautiful cards, especially the hand-painted ones from the children.

As I broke the bread and gave her a drop of communion wine the three of us were enveloped by a tremendous sense of peace. Despite her frailty, Rita sat up in bed and gave a small wave as I left the room. I knew it was the last time I would see her alive.

Rita's funeral service took place one sunny Friday in May. I told a packed church all about her faith, her courage and her hopes and how, even though she was no longer with us, she would continue to help others through the small library at the back of the church which contained her favourite books.

At the end of the service I told everyone it was Rita's dying wish that all donations at her funeral should go to the Children's Society.

That afternoon Ann took part in her school's cross-country race. She was disappointed not to win, but several onlookers cheered her for being a pretty good runner-up.

I bent down to kiss Ann goodnight. "Never mind," I said light-heartedly. "There's always next time."

Just then I noticed the book she'd been reading – *The Small Woman: The Story of Gladys Aylward.*

"It's a good book, dad, have you read it?"

I told her I had, and asked how she'd got hold of it.

"One evening when I went for a practice run I felt a bit tired and rested for a few minutes in Combe Peter Church. That's where I found it."

I picked it up. Inside the cover I read the words 'To Steve, with all my love, Rita'.

I passed the book back to Ann with a warm smile.

What better end could there be to the day of Rita's funeral?

Chapter 16

A Costly Pearl

First it was dustbins being kicked over at night; next stones were being thrown at windows; then a furious Len Cooksley reported that Ashenridge church gate had been daubed with bright-red paint.

Of course, everybody knew who was responsible. A twelve-year-old boy named Alf Harris who, like others of his ilk, had the knack of putting on such an innocent expression that he got away with blue murder. You couldn't really call him a delinquent – more a pain in the neck.

Nonetheless, from a tiny piece of grit a magnificent pearl can grow – a painful process for the poor oyster in whose shell this transformation takes place. In our case the pearl was Alf – the poor oyster our youth club.

All that had happened two years ago. The police had been informed but had far more serious offences to deal with. To them a vandalised church gate was hardly a priority. Roy Edwards, my curate at the time, was convinced that if we took a different line and tried to understand Alf we could change him. I wasn't so sure.

That Whitsun James Bearne, a friend of Roy's, supported by a handful of students, organised a children's mission which we referred to as the Holiday Club.

It began on the Saturday morning when twelve rather self-conscious youngsters arrived at Brookworthy Parish Hall. They played several games, sang some lively choruses, then James asked the children to sit down while he told them his version of the Feeding of the Five Thousand. The children were spellbound.

Twelve went home for lunch, but when the club opened that afternoon twenty children appeared. Two days later forty turned up.

I looked in on them one afternoon and was amazed to see Alf Harris and his pals there sitting alongside one of the leaders and chatting away quite happily. When they noticed me they were keen to tell me about the games that had filled most of their morning. They'd obviously had a good time.

Later Roy told me a little more. One evening he happened to come across Alf and his friends who were hanging around Ashenridge church gate. They got talking and as a result Alf and his pals had cycled over to Brookworthy and actually helped with the games. He lingered on after the other children had left and even stayed for the team prayer and praise meeting. Roy assured me there was a very different side to Alf, especially when he was away from his friends.

Roy hoped I would give him a chance and not simply write him off as a troublemaker. I promised I would.

Two years later Roy had moved to another parish, but James and his team returned to organise another Holiday Club. This time they based their activities at Ashenridge Rectory. Things did not bode well. Nowadays Alf and his so-called friends preferred to sit around and laugh at people rather than get involved in activities which they regarded as juvenile.

In keeping with the times, Alf had had his hair cut in the style of The Beatles. This must surely have met with disapproval at school, but it certainly enhanced his status with his peers, who immediately copied him.

He regarded church as 'kid's stuff', and made fun of the children who attended. One Sunday he and his friends were making a lot of noise outside the church while the service was in progress. I wondered what he would do about the forthcoming Holiday Club? I was about to find out!

On the first morning sixty children arrived complete with packed lunches, spare clothes and pocket money for the tuck shop. Mary and Paul ran the tuck shop, always a favourite at Holiday Club. The children were greeted by a team of some fifteen students led by James with extra help coming from Cedric, Will Swift and myself.

The children were divided into age groups and then teams to play games in the field. Afterwards we gathered in a packed hall for lively singing and fun with puppets. Then all went quiet as James told one of his favourite Bible stories – Jacob's Ladder. Until then there'd been no sign of Alf, who probably considered himself far too old for the games, but he now appeared in the hall and listened intently to the story.

Unfortunately, he and his friends made their presence felt again that afternoon only seconds after we'd started playing a popular game called 'flags'. Loud horns were being blown non-stop, they started calling people rude names, and finally missiles were thrown over the hedge. James slipped away to have a quiet word with them.

We saw no more of them until seven-thirty when they joined us for the evening session – a game of football involving twenty teenage boys and girls. Their silly behaviour ruined the game and when it was time to go home we could still hear them making rude noises in the shrubbery.

After the last of the children had gone, the team met for hot drinks and prayers in our drawing-room. They may have felt tired, but the problems we'd encountered demanded strong faith and I was impressed by the quality of their praying.

My heart sank when Alf and his friends turned up again the next day. However, they seemed content to look on and occasionally leant a hand. How long would that last, I wondered? They stayed behind for the talk but left before the evening service. I was impressed with the gentle way James dealt with them, and later that evening a tired but happy team gave heartfelt thanks to God for a really good day.

By Friday nearly one hundred children were coming along to the Holiday Club – more than we could ever have expected. As the week went on a small miracle happened. The children simply changed. They started asking Cedric and me all sorts of deep questions about prayer, faith, even life after death. We seemed to be meeting on equal terms. He may not have liked the noisy choruses we sang, but for the first time in his life Cedric discovered he enjoyed working with children. They liked him and he liked them. God had performed something very special that week.

Alf and his friends had become helpful enough, which was a step in the right direction, but not for the first time I wondered how long it would last.

After the last evening of the Holiday Club we all sank into our beds utterly exhausted. I was drifting into a lovely sleep, going over all the happy events of the week, when the phone rang. It was Annie Cook. "I don't like to disturb you so late, Mr Longfield, but something funny's going on at the top of the church tower."

I silently cursed Annie. We'd been having problems with pigeons in the tower and I suspected this was a false alarm. I quickly put a dressing gown over my pyjamas, stuck my feet in a pair of slippers and grabbed a torch. Mary was sound asleep and there was no point in waking her.

The church was unlocked and, more worryingly, so was the door leading to the tower. But then it wouldn't be the first time Len had forgotten to lock up for the night. The ringing chamber was empty, the bell ropes undisturbed. As I shone my torch upwards there was a rustling and a frightened pigeon flew out of the tower window. The silly bird startled me, but I was relieved that everything else seemed all right. My relief was short-lived when I became aware of the smell of paint. Where was it coming from?

I supposed it wouldn't do any harm to check the tower while I was there. At least I could put Annie's mind at rest. Holding on to the torch with one hand and grasping the rail with the other, I struggled to the top and again found nothing untoward. It was only when I swung the torch round that the beam picked out three figures cowering against the battlements. I nearly dropped the torch in fright, but quickly recognised the three figures as none other than Alf's pals. They didn't look so brave now. They were holding on to each other for grim death and one of them was clutching a tin of paint.

Where was Alf? I swung the torch upwards and could just make out a ladder propped against one of the pinnacles. Alf was balanced at the very top. It would have been the end if he'd fallen.

After all we'd done over the last week, was this how he repaid us, spreading paint all over the top of the tower? I shouted at him to come down at once and as his feet touched the floor of the tower he found his voice and falteringly tried to explain.

"Honest, Mr Longfield, we didn't mean any harm. We wanted to thank you for all the fun we had last week. It was that story James Bearne told us, you know the one about Jacob's ladder. He said it came from the Book of Geniuses. My dad once told me I was a bit of a genius. And then I heard you making a joke afterwards about the ladder in your tower and how the weather vane on top of the church could do with a lick of paint. We only wanted to thank you for all the games and things."

I didn't know whether to laugh or cry. One false move and Alf would have fallen to certain death. I could see that in his own way Alf was telling the truth. I also understood that in his eyes performing such a dangerous act meant he could still come to the Holiday Club and be thought of as a man.

Perhaps it was sheer folly on my part, but I had seen God at work more than once during that week. I put my trust in him now, tested the ladder and took the paint brush out of Alf's hand. A few hasty strokes and the job was done.

As we manoeuvred the ladder back into the bell chamber I assured all four boys that, providing they promised never to do such a foolhardy thing again, I would not split on them. I left it to them to think of a convincing story to tell their parents. I had to think of an equally convincing way to satisfy Annie Cook.

As for Alf, he never became a regular worshipper. He'd turn up for the occasional service and never missed Christingle. As he grew into manhood he struggled to strike a balance between being a lad with the lads and being a Christian. I suspect he didn't find it easy.

Some years later a local clergyman told me a story about Alf, his regular window cleaner, who one day started quizzing him about his church. The vicar asked him why he was so interested?

"Because I'm a Christian," Alf had replied in a matter of fact voice. "When I was a teenager I used to go to the Holiday Club at Ashenridge."

Chapter 17

Beware of the Drive

We could hear Ann's penetrating screams as she came flying along the drive. "Mum, dad, there's been a terrible accident. Come quickly, it's Paul."

Mary threw down the tea towel and we charged through the front door together fearing the worst.

Paul was spread-eagled on the drive, blood pouring from his head, his buckled bicycle lying on top of him. Through her sobs Ann managed to explain that the front wheel of the bike had gone into a pothole and Paul had been catapulted over the handlebars.

Because of my training in the royal Army Medical Corps I knew what to do instinctively, but all the same my heart was thumping nineteen to the dozen and my hands were shaking as I examined Paul. I couldn't find any broken bones, and the cut on his forehead looked worse than it was, but I was still in two minds whether to ring for a doctor. My relief when Paul opened his eyes was unimaginable, and both Ann and Mary, who had been clutching each other in silence, now started crying.

Between us we carried Paul back to the house and laid him on a settee in the drawing-room. A cold compress helped to stem the flow of blood and Paul was all for going out again, but Mary insisted he should stay where he was for the rest of the morning.

"Sorry, dad. Couldn't have been looking where I was going. Hope I haven't made a dent in the drive?" It was just like Paul to crack a joke in the midst of all this drama.

There was no denying it, the potholes in the rectory drive were getting bigger and deeper and we all knew that sooner or later they would lead to a crisis.

Every time we had bad weather more chunks of asphalt broke away leaving great holes. I filled them in with ash from the Rayburn, but every time it rained we were back to square one. As a result, dangerous gaping holes awaited the unwary, especially on dark evenings. Poor Annie Cook had already taken a tumble some weeks ago, and although it wasn't serious and she hadn't made a fuss about it, Mrs Mathilda Pink had no hesitation in telling me: "You're lucky it was Annie. Someone else might have prosecuted you."

Paul's accident had brought things to a head and we could no longer ignore the fact that accidents were bound to happen if something wasn't done about the drive.

The only reason I'd hesitated before taking action was because I knew that once I contacted the diocese it would inevitably lead to yet another battle about the future of the rectory. But I had no choice now and rang the Diocesan

Parsonages Board knowing I'd probably be opening up a can of worms.

All clergy property is inspected every five years by a surveyor appointed by the diocese. It's his job to go round making a list of all the repairs needed and to ensure that they are carried out. I'd been hoping the drive would last until the next official inspection for two good reasons.

Firstly, the diocese had little patience with moaning clergy who constantly complained about their houses. The second, and more serious reason, was because the church had developed a policy of replacing older houses like our rectory with smaller modern ones. That might be fine in parishes where there are plenty of church rooms. Here there were none, and even if it had been available, the well-used parish hall was not really suitable for the many small meetings which we held at the rectory.

As the Badger Group had grown in size and scope, the spacious rectory had become very much a centre for my work as well as being a home. Confirmation classes, church councils, home study Bible groups, all manner of meetings took place there. What a loss if the rectory were to be replaced by the kind of house the authorities preferred. Drawing their attention to expensive issues like resurfacing the drive would only strengthen their case to dispose of it.

Three days later I received a visit from the diocesan surveyor. He could see straight away that resurfacing was the only answer. The problem was the cost involved. He knew what the diocese would say – if constant use by the parishioners was contributing to the wear and tear on the drive then they should contribute to the cost of repairs.

His estimate for the job came out at £300. He warned me that when his report went through it would almost certainly prompt the diocese to discuss the disposal of the rectory. He asked if there was any way in which we could raise half the amount, which might encourage them to be a little more sympathetic.

Ironically, parishioners who were keen to raise hundreds of pounds for church buildings felt very differently when it came to the rectory. There was nothing personal in this, but many could remember the church selling off redundant rectories in other parishes and seemingly pocketing the money.

It took all my energy to persuade the Badger Group that we should organise a Group Coffee Morning. In the end they gave way, and a fortnight later posters went up in all six parishes.

I'd been put in a very embarrassing position by the diocese. Who else has to go begging for money to repair a drive? Embarrassed, hurt, angry, I prayed about it in church that morning. Some days I seemed to have a hot line to God and my prayers were clearly answered. On other occasions I felt I was holding on to a very slender thread of faith. That day it seemed as if God wanted to slay me, as the Psalmist once put it.

As if things weren't bad enough, Mary's cousin, Will, chose this critical moment to pay an unexpected visit which was nearly our undoing.

Mary and I had no idea that Will's affairs had collapsed yet again. Whatever he turned his hand to you could bank on it being short-lived and Will would find himself penniless – although somehow he always managed to find enough to buy a drop or two of alcohol with which to drown his sorrows. No wonder he remained written off as the black sheep of Mary's family. In times of trouble he always turned to us for help – no one else in the family wanted to know him.

Having got as far as Leighford, Will proceeded to spend the last of his money in the local hostelry where, it being market day, he inevitably bumped into my number one enemy, Peter Eastridge. Knowing Will of old, Peter plied him with endless drinks and after a couple of raucous hours at the bar told Will he'd be more than happy to give him a lift to the rectory.

"When you gets there, mind the parson's drive. 'Tis full of 'oles."

Will chortled away to himself. "Parshon's drive. Potholsh! He'sh not going to need that much longer. He'sh worth a dozen mishups. He'sh a good man...He'll be one soon....a mishup.... no did I say mishup, I mean bishup. Ha! Ha! Ha!"

Peter laughed along with him. This really was good news. Jack Longfield being made a bishop. At last the dreadful parson would be gone and nothing could stop Peter becoming a churchwarden. He knew all about the reputation of the man he was taking home, and now he'd got him in his car wondered what else could he pump out of the silly old sot? How much more dirt could he rake up? He needed time to prod, so he decided to take a roundabout way home.

"'E's going to become a bishop, eh?" asked Peter craftily. "When's all this goin' to 'appen?"

"He hashn't told me that....any day now....I hope he doeshn't trip over his holes."

"I s'pose 'e's got lots of friends in 'igh places that'll pull a few strings?"

"I don't know about that. Ha! Ha! He won't have any potholsh then, not once he'sh living in a palash."

"So you'm going to celebrate with 'im tonight? I bet 'e can put the pints away?"

"No, he doeshn't know I'm coming. He won't like it if he thinksh I've been shelebrating. You won't...will you?"

"Won't what?"

"Who...won't...what?"

Much to Peter's disappointment, Will passed out, and he was left with a loudly-snoring passenger. When they arrived at the rectory he struggled to wake Will from his drunken slumber, and getting him out of the car was no mean feat.

Poor Will was left to fumble and stumble his way along the dark, potholed drive whilst a scheming Peter Eastridge drove off, a look of triumph all over his face.

As usual, Paul and Ann were in a tearing hurry to catch the school bus and we'd only just said goodbye when they came bursting through the door again.

"Dad, you're not going to believe this." Paul could hardly get the words out.

"We've just seen Uncle Tiddly. He's asleep on the back seat of your car. I banged on the window but he didn't move. I think he could be dead."

Will certainly was not dead. He was very much alive, stretched half in and half out of the car, a battered straw hat squashed down over his eyes. Mary turned on her heel and walked back to the rectory in disgust. Paul and Ann were laughing their heads off and I told them to get off to school right away. I was left inhaling fumes that were enough to knock me out.

Putting on a supreme effort, as if he was a celebrity stepping out to be greeted by a crowd of admirers, Will raised his arms towards the trees and proclaimed: "Just passing, exploring new avenues of commerce in this glorious part of England. Couldn't pass your door without looking in. Knew how hurt you'd be if I didn't..."

I pointed to the car: "How long have you been in there?"

"Must confess I did arrive a little late last night. Couldn't disturb you. Thought I'd wait until it was a decent time to call."

"From closing time until eight o'clock. And meantime you've made my car stink like a brewery."

"You know, Jack, your drive is awfully dangerous. I nearly killed myself. Look at those terrible holes. I'm surprised the bishop hasn't done something about it. By the way, I didn't know you and Mary had a dog?"

"We haven't got a dog."

"Then what's the point of having a sign at the bottom of your drive saying 'beware of the dog'?"

This was nothing short of a Brian Rix farce, but I wasn't laughing. Sure enough, some joker had propped a sign at the side of our entrance and it did say 'beware of the dog', but Will had failed to notice the word 'dog' had been scratched out with chalk and replaced with the word 'drive'.

Will managed to consume half a loaf of bread and all the marmalade we had in the house. Mary let me know her feelings by leaving me alone with her errant cousin. I left him briefly to deal with a couple of phone calls, but by the time I'd finished he was sound asleep in the armchair. No point in waking him, better to let him sleep it off, again.

I had some very peculiar conversations that morning. On my way to the village shop I was warmly greeted by the ladies in the bus shelter. There were smiles all round and I found myself being heartily congratulated.

Yes, I told them, it was good to know that people were pleased the drive would be made safe. For some reason my remark met with an awkward silence. They then seemed to recover and asked if it would be happening soon? I warned them that things like this didn't usually happen overnight. Making the most of the opportunity, I encouraged them to get everybody to support the coffee morning. That would help to speed things up.

One of the ladies wondered if we'd still need the coffee morning, but Kitty shut her up and said she must be thinking of something else. I left the group in silence, but had only gone a few yards before they all began arguing at the same time.

Mr Radd at the village shop greeted me with a knowing smile, but gave no hint as to what it was all about. Indeed, everywhere I went smiles seemed to be the order of the day. Something odd was going on!

It was only when I eventually arrived at the church that the story unfolded. Hearing me come in, a head popped up from under one of the pews.

"What's up, Len?" I asked. "Have you lost something?"

"In a way I 'ave, sir," he replied. Again I was greeted with one of those knowing smiles.

"So, what's missing?"

"Tis one of they 'aydge boars. I seed 'un 'ere when I fust comed in, but tidn't 'ere now." Then, giving me that same smile again, he continued: "But that'll not be worryin' you now, sir. You'm mindin' better things than that now."

I was so curious about the 'aydge boars I missed his second point and asked him again what he was looking for?

"Told you, one of they 'aydge boars," he repeated impatiently.

I hadn't a clue what he was talking about and he went into one of his complicated explanations. "You knows what I means. One of they things like a brish, only they'm round and they'm full of fleas. They'm a proper nuisance. People don't like they in church."

Having lived in the West Country for nearly ten years I thought I knew most country expressions, but I had to admit this one had me beaten.

Still seeing me struggle Len said in an exasperated tone: "You knows, they normally lives in 'aydges. They'm prickly an' gets run over on they roads."

The penny dropped. "Got you, Len. Hedgehogs. Let me help you look."

"No thank you, sir, not now."

"Why not now?"

Standing upright he declared: "You'm much too important now to be lookin' for 'aydge boars."

"What on earth do you mean, Len?"

Looking me straight in the eye, and with an air of affectation only he could pull off, Len said: "Why, you knows what they'm all sayin', you'm goin' to leave us to become...*a bishop*."

I nearly collapsed. Bit by bit Len told me the story as he'd heard it. Having got Will well and truly drunk, Peter Eastridge had driven him home to Ashenridge, and hearing Will talk some silly nonsense about me being a bishop put two and two together and wasted no time in spreading the news around the village.

Len's parting shot was that everybody now supposed the fund raising event for repairing the drive would be cancelled. I told him it most certainly would not.

Will hadn't moved an inch. Mary had looked in on him a couple of times and been greeted with loud snoring. I'd had enough. I marched in and woke him up unceremoniously.

"How dare you, Will. How dare you spread rumours about me becoming a bishop. And to Peter Eastridge of all people."

Will recalled little of his conversation with Peter. What he did remember was all about potholes. He admitted he may have said I was worth so many bishops, but flatly denied saying I was about to become one. I could well imagine Peter Eastridge had been putting words into his mouth.

"Jack, I'm truly sorry if I've given anyone the wrong impression. You know what I'm like when I've had a drink or two."

Will now put on a pathetically pleading look and got down to the real reason for his visit. As he spoke I began to weaken and felt obliged to help. He may have his faults, but underneath that blustery exterior lay a good man who unfortunately seemed destined to attract bad luck.

I reassured Will we would not throw him out, and after a heated discussion with Mary said he was welcome to stay – providing he did not go near the village.

When Paul and Ann came home, they were delighted to see their naughty Uncle Tiddly was still with us, and very amused when he told them about his latest escapade. Now they were that much older I wondered if Uncle Tiddly would have the same appeal, but he was a good actor and had no trouble adjusting his repertoire.

I spent the rest of the day putting the record straight with Cedric and the various churchwardens. Even if Peter Eastridge's rumours were now known to be untrue, he had succeeded in stirring up yet more resentment over running a coffee morning for repairs to the drive. More and more people were holding forth about the church profiteering from redundant rectories.

Taking advice from several of the churchwardens, we decided to hold an emergency meeting at the rectory the following evening.

Unfortunately, there was confusion over the time of this meeting. Hardly had I finished tea when the Westaleigh churchwardens arrived twenty minutes before anyone else. Tom Short had a long tale to tell about a deceased former resident whose family wanted him to be brought back and buried in the churchyard. Meanwhile, Sir William Radlett, realising he was early, diplomatically went for a walk in the garden. While Tom was talking to me I could hear the unmistakable voice of Will holding forth to his namesake. I desperately wanted to get Will out of the way before he did any more harm, but Tom's story was both urgent and complicated and there was no way I could cut him short without appearing rude.

Tom went into the entire history of the bereaved family. I could hear snatches of conversation from the garden. A theatrical voice was talking about 'cash shortfalls', 'commercial enterprises', 'the Queen'. I even overheard the dreaded word 'bishop'. Will seemed to be doing all the talking. Was he trying some hard luck story on Sir William? If he was, I knew I would hear about it in no uncertain terms once the meeting was over.

There was a lot of plain speaking at the meeting. Talk about my leaving was soon dismissed, but people had been thinking long and hard about the main issue. Led by Colonel Waters we decided that if the diocese wanted to add further parishes to the group, which would entail selling more redundant rectories, we would only agree on condition that the surviving clergy houses be put in tip-top order. People had great sympathy with my plight, and hoped I would never again be expected to go to the parishes cap in hand.

According to Will, Sir William Radlett's old firm happened to be looking for a representative. Sir William had taken a liking to Will and was sure he'd be the right man for the job. Will was to travel to London for an interview the day before the coffee morning.

The coffee morning was still going to take a lot of selling. People were finding it hard to persuade their friends to come. On the basis that there is no smoke without fire, many who believed I was not going to be made a bishop were convinced I was about to leave the parish. It even got the thumbs down from the ladies in the bus shelter, until Annie Cook managed to persuade them to think again.

Cedric did his best to encourage the people in Westaleigh and Brookworthy. They were polite about it, but he guessed from their evasive answers that few would come

On the Friday afternoon Mary and I were down at the hall working with others to prepare the stalls. At least some people seemed to have taken pity on us and there were more helpers than we'd expected. In fact I got so absorbed I forgot I was taking Will to catch the bus at Leighford – our railway had by now fallen under the Beeching Axe. Not wanting to miss the interview, Will broke his promise and appeared at the hall.

In his best stage voice, which nobody in the hall could possibly miss, he told us that while we were out the 'archbishop' – he meant archdeacon – had rung to say that we need not bother to raise any money after all. The diocese would carry out the necessary repairs and had decided to build a brand-new house for us in part of the rectory garden. The archdeacon knew we'd be delighted with this news.

Before Mary or I had a chance to say anything everyone began packing up their things to go home.

I drove Will to the bus in near silence. I could hardly blame him for innocently passing on what he thought was good news. I wished him good luck and he promised to let me know the result of the interview.

Mary was nowhere to be seen when I got back to the rectory. I knew how desperately sad she would be and I wanted to be with her. Reluctantly I returned to the hall expecting to find Mary alone, abandoned by all the other helpers.

To my amazement the hall was buzzing with activity. Mary drew me aside and explained what had happened.

Mrs Mathilda Pink was in the kitchen and overheard Will passing on the message from the archdeacon. She came back into the hall just after I had left and was flabbergasted to see everyone packing up and getting ready to go home. When told the reason why she became incensed and addressed the entire room at the top of her voice.

"How dare they. How dare they do away with the rectory. Not one of them has taken the trouble to find out how much it is used. We won't let them get away with it. We'll shame them. We'll raise so much money they'll never have the nerve to carry out their threat."

This was Mathilda Pink at her most formidable. Her words spread like wildfire round all six parishes, and the parishioners were more determined than ever to make their protest felt by the diocese.

The coffee morning proved to be an outstanding success.

Chapter 18

Making My Life a Misery

Something was seriously wrong. Cedric's smile had vanished, he'd stopped confiding in me, and he no longer accepted invitations to share meals with us at the rectory. We still worshipped together and discussed practical matters at our Monday morning meetings, but that was as far as it went. Had I done something wrong? Was it my fault?

Perhaps Cedric needed someone with whom he could share his life. There were plenty of suitable young ladies in and around our parishes, but every time the subject came up he vowed he was a confirmed bachelor. Mary and I had often wondered if he'd been put off marriage when his parents divorced.

I was mulling this over one afternoon while working in the garden. I'd been heaping grass and hedge trimmings for over a month, but heavy rainfalls had prevented me from having a bonfire. A period of strong easterly winds meant I could finish the job at last – just one match and the bonfire was well and truly alight. I had an uncanny feeling Cedric's problems might flare up in the same way. Unfortunately they did, and in more ways than one.

Cedric was taking the Sunday service at Ashenridge and during his sermon implied that those who believed in the healing miracles of the New Testament were fools.

The whole congregation was up in arms, and Will Swift, the churchwarden, was close to walking out of the service. Will was no narrow-minded fundamentalist – indeed he was studying a wide range of theological beliefs with a view to becoming a lay reader – but he considered Cedric had overstepped the mark.

After the service he challenged Cedric, who in turn accused Will of being even more gullible than me when it came to the subject of miracles.

Not only was Will angry that he'd made such a dismissive remark about me behind my back; he also feared Cedric was alienating a lot of people with his scepticism.

Will blamed it on the tiny group who met with Cedric at Westaleigh Vicarage each week. He referred to them as 'egg heads' because they prided themselves in being intellectuals. Will happened to know one of them, a young man who openly boasted that most of them did not believe in God.

Will told Cedric in no uncertain terms he should be listening to me rather than to them.

I was worried, too, because Cedric seemed to regard himself as being on a far higher intellectual plane than most ordinary Christians. I'd taken him to task over it on several occasions, but he insisted I was making a fuss about nothing.

The flames were fanned further with the arrival in Ashenridge of a rather forbidding lady by the name of Miss Pringle. I first heard about her from one of my fellow clergy in Whiteminster.

"How lucky you are," he assured me. "She'll be a real asset to your church. She's one of the bishop's long-standing friends. A lovely lady, but it'll take you a while to get to know her."

I looked forward to meeting Miss Pringle. She'd arrived in Ashenridge at the time the fiasco over our drive was taking place and my visit to her was long overdue. I did not receive a warm welcome.

"Do you know, Mr Longfield, I've been living here a fortnight now and not one person from Ashenridge Church has bothered to call."

All six feet of a disapproving Miss Pringle stood before me. Her large hands were those of a woman who knew what she wanted and got it. She wore severe-looking spectacles on the end of her nose and her smile, if you could call it a smile, was decidedly frosty.

For someone so new to the parish, Miss Pringle had managed to accumulate an extraordinary stream of complaints which she now reeled off.

She had not attended church because the times were inconvenient. She preferred an early morning Communion service, not a short one after Matins. She was not very impressed by what she had seen. She had looked in at the church one Tuesday morning, which happened to be St Peter's day. To her disgust there was no service; even worse, the altar hangings were the incorrect colour. As for the flowers, they looked half-dead. She liked quiet, dignified services, restrained music, and most certainly would not tolerate noisy children in church.

When I managed to get a word in she was by no means satisfied by my explanations. Whatever I said was brushed aside. Evidently any attempt to reform a hopeless country clergyman like me would be a waste of time. Cedric, on the other hand, was numbered as one of her elect – I didn't even know they had met.

"Your curate is a charming young man. You could learn a thing or two from him."

Perhaps I could, but between them Cedric and Miss Pringle seemed determined to make my life a misery!

One of the problems of a parish church is providing for the differing tastes of the people it serves. Some churches may ignore this and only cater for a limited circle who enjoy the same type of service every week. This might benefit the Miss Pringles of this world but would probably leave nearly everyone else out in the cold.

Yes, it can work in towns where there is a choice of churches, each catering for a different taste in worship, but in villages where there is only one church things have to be flexible. I was well aware that not every one of our services pleased everybody, but I did what I believed was right, and my Church Councils supported me.

It was most unfortunate that the first service Miss Pringle attended was definitely not to her liking. I'd been delayed at Combe Peter helping someone with a pressing problem and arrived a little late for the Family Service at Ashenridge. Much to my surprise I found Miss Pringle sitting just inside the door. She made a point of looking at her watch, turned to me with a look of disapproval, then glared at the fidgeting children. She was going to have a field day and I suspected she would collar me after the service.

We began with a rousing hymn – not at all to Miss Pringle's taste. I might have shunned this style of music myself, and the informality of the service which followed, but years ago my first curate had changed my rather fusty ideas. Thanks to him this rather relaxed style of service was now firmly established and we could still bank on it attracting the largest congregation each month.

I was always at pains to point out that the Family Service was not just a children's service, there was something in it for all ages. It was particularly satisfying to see so many of the older ones enjoying it.

The Sunday School children formed a group with their teacher and sang 'Wide wide as the ocean', and where appropriate stretched their arms wide, deep or high to fit in with the words. Most of the congregation joined in. Miss Pringle's mouth remained firmly shut and her arms stayed firmly by her side.

When it came to the address, I invited some of the children to mime the first part of the story with me. Little Billy, who was acting the part of the lost sheep, made a beeline for Miss Pringle's pew and hid underneath it baaing loudly. Eventually the shepherd found him and took him home to the rest of the flock. I half expected a shocked Miss Pringle to storm out, but she was made of sterner stuff. No doubt she was keeping a mental record of all my wrongdoings, just like the Pharisees of old.

Nobody was going to stop me now. After the address came the main point I wanted to make. It was hard hitting but I knew it applied to all of us in church, no matter what our age.

I spoke of the sufferings of the shepherd rescuing the sheep and followed this with a heart-breaking story about a group of missionaries who were martyred as they tried to reach God's lost people. They gave their lives telling others about their faith, so why should we be afraid of a little mockery from our own doubting friends.

At the end of the service Miss Pringle gave me a look of contempt before making a hasty exit. I could have sworn she muttered something about going back to kindergarten.

A distressed Will Swift came to see me a few days later. He'd bumped into Miss Pringle whilst out on his daily walk and from the way she spoke it seemed as though she had become a rallying point for anyone with a grouse against me. There was one ray of hope. She assured Will she had a reputation for being fair.

Miss Pringle was delighted to learn there would be an early-morning Communion service the following Sunday, and even more delighted when she heard that Cedric would be taking it. He arrived in good time, kept to every word normally used from the Prayer Book, and paused at the right moments.

After the service she invited him to join her for coffee. Cedric felt flattered, especially when she compared his service much more favourably to mine the week before.

Next morning Miss Pringle arrived without warning at the rectory. She was anxious to talk about Cedric. At last he had found in her a sympathetic, mother-like figure in whom he could confide. He told her how unwell and depressed he felt, how his ministry was getting nowhere. He even admitted he'd allowed himself to be influenced by a small group of sceptical friends. He felt guilty, too, knowing he'd been two-faced and regretted talking behind my back to the likes of Peter Eastridge. And he realised it had been naive of him to listen to the churchwardens at Westaleigh when they tried to persuade him to become the vicar there and abandon the Badger Group.

At least I now knew for certain that Cedric was unwell, but couldn't help wondering why he hadn't turned to me for help. Miss Pringle feared he would leave the ministry and decided her dear friend, the bishop, must be involved, and sooner rather than later.

Looking as severe as ever, and refusing the cup of coffee Mary offered her, Miss Pringle confessed she had now gained a much better idea of all my responsibilities, added to which parishioners had not been slow in coming to my defence.

Miss Pringle gave nothing away and concluded by saying: "I am sorry to press myself on you like this, but I've uncovered some serious problems. Believe it or not I'm acting in your best interests by contacting the bishop."

Noticing my look of concern she continued, without a hint of a smile: "I'm afraid you'll have to get used to me, Mr Longfield. I'm a bit of an acquired taste."

My heart sank. I liked the bishop, but his friends were another matter. I felt angry about Miss Pringle's interference. What right had she to act like this having lived here only a matter of weeks? I called after her to find out what she had in mind, but she strode off without another word.

From that moment on events moved into top gear. On my advice, Cedric did see the bishop and made a clean breast of everything. On the strength of this the bishop rang saying he would like to visit in a week's time. Furthermore, he would value an opportunity to speak to the members of the various Church Councils at a joint meeting. He was concerned about the future, but assured me he had some very positive ideas. I offered to arrive a little later so that people would not feel inhibited when talking to him, but he would not countenance it. He did, however, make a special request that Miss Pringle be at the meeting.

Peter Eastridge was furious. He'd been invited on more than one occasion to join the Church Council, but always refused saying he would only do so if we made him a churchwarden. Because of that he'd now miss a golden opportunity to meet the bishop, but I had no doubts he would find a way of getting his objections voiced.

Sir William Radlett, in his usual frank manner, warned me that since we were now six parishes he would be renewing his demand for Westaleigh to be an independent parish with Cedric as its vicar.

The prospect of a visit from the bishop caused great excitement. I let it be known that he would want to discuss the future of the rectory and the parishes and would like to hear other people's ideas. Rumours were rife. Some thought I might be given the sack, others assumed churches would be closed and the Badger Group disbanded, and so on.

That Saturday morning Len Cooksley popped in to warn me there were problems over the booking of Ashenridge Parish Hall. While he was talking I could hardly take my eyes off his feet. Screaming at me from the space between his turn-ups and his shoes were brilliant orange football socks.

"Us came to say they won' be to 'Erb's farm come Tuesday. The fruit ain't ready yet, so they'm goin' to impoverish something, only t'won't be to 'Erb's. 'E 'asn't 'nuff seats, so they 'ad to change their 'tentions an' come 'ere instead."

I couldn't understand a word of what he was saying and Len tried again: "Come Tuesday they'll all be 'ere. 'Erb 'asn't 'nuff seats. Only us thought you'd best know. Erb knowed 'is plums weren't ripe for they to use."

I nodded and hoped I'd got the message right. It sounded like some of the Church Councillors, instead of making jam on Herb's farm, would be coming to our meeting because he did not have enough seats.

I thanked Len, but couldn't let him go without asking about the socks.

"Why, 'twas to the Over Sixties sale to Leighford last Wednesday. Us bought four pairs of they – only cost me a shillin'. Good ain't they?"

At the end of my Sunday sermon I gave out a quick reminder regarding the bishop's visit on Tuesday. I could have sworn I heard a grunt coming from Len and it wasn't until the end of the service that he approached me supported by two stalwarts from the Women's Institute.

Was I not aware they had already booked Ashenridge Parish Hall for that very evening? They always met there on a particular Tuesday in the month, and now they were no longer making jam at Herb's farm would be using it for an improvised meeting.

I managed to warn the congregation before they left about the change of venue. We had no choice now but to go to the parish hall at Brookworthy, which would mean a whole evening sitting on uncomfortable wooden benches. Unbeknown to me Mrs Batchelor, who was not wearing her hearing aid, left the church without having heard one word of my message.

The atmosphere that day was tense with excitement. People were preparing their party pieces. Peter Eastridge, still sore that he was excluded from the meeting, took comfort in the fact that the bishop wanted Miss Pringle to attend – she would be an excellent spokesman for him. Will Swift and others were prepared to come to my defence if I came in for heavy criticism. It promised to be an interesting evening.

The bishop wasn't due until four o'clock and I was helping Mary prepare tea when the door bell rang. It was Cedric's brother, Steven Palmer. I could tell straight away something was horribly wrong. His pale face was screwed up in anxiety and he grabbed hold of my arm. "It's Cedric. I can't wake him. I only arrived this afternoon and found him on the bedroom floor. You're not going to like this, I think he's drunk!"

Chapter 19

Life's Full of Surprises

Cedric was lying half-naked on the bedroom floor, an empty bottle of Blue Nun by his side. He may have been drunk, but my practised eye told me there was more to it than that. He looked ill. His colour was all wrong, his pulse was weak and he had a slight fever.

He was only wearing the top half of his pyjamas, the buttons still undone. The bottom half lay beside him on the floor. I noticed a half-empty bottle of painkillers on the dressing table but had no way of knowing how many tablets, if any, Cedric had taken.

"Steven, call for an ambulance, now!" The urgency with which I said it had him flying downstairs and I could hear him making the call.

"Said they'll be here in about fifteen minutes." Steven gave me an agonized look. "He is going to be all right, isn't he?"

Before I could answer Cedric groaned and started grasping his side. I put gentle pressure on the spot then quickly took my hand away. Cedric let out an ear-splitting yell and half opened his eyes. "Sorry, Jack. Sorry for getting things wrong. Not been feeling too well just lately."

"Don't worry about that now, Cedric. We're going to get you into hospital. They'll soon sort you out. Can you tell me how many tablets you've taken?"

"Can't remember. But I want you to know how sorry I am. Sorry for what I said behind your back...sorry for being weak...sorry for being afraid to face up to this evening's meeting."

He was getting himself worked up and I prayed that the ambulance would arrive quickly.

The journey to Whiteminster General seemed to take a lifetime. I went in the ambulance with Cedric and Steven followed in his car. I prayed the ambulance crew wouldn't switch the siren on knowing that could mean only one thing. I also prayed the traffic in the city wouldn't delay us.

Steven and I sat in a side room drinking endless cups of tea while the doctors deliberated. I wasn't surprised when they diagnosed Cedric as having acute appendicitis, but without knowing how much alcohol he'd drunk or how many painkillers he'd taken they couldn't risk operating straight away. There was a slight risk of peritonitis, but under the circumstances all they could do was keep him stable until it was safe to operate.

I rang Mary and explained it was unlikely I'd be back in time for tea with the bishop – at this stage I didn't even know if I'd be back in time for the meeting.

As we sat there Steven opened up to me. Theirs hadn't been the happiest of childhoods. Living in an unhappy environment with cold, unfeeling parents, Cedric and Steven had turned to each other more and more and as they grew up became very close. Of course, they differed over many things, but always shared their deepest feelings.

How different Steven was to the last time we met. He still wore that dreadful Maoist cap – I wondered if it ever left his head – but he was speaking to me now like a trusted friend.

"I don't suppose Cedric ever mentioned his first love to you?"

I shook my head. "He only ever told me he was a confirmed bachelor. Nothing about a girl in his life."

"He fell deeply in love with the daughter of a Baptist minister. Eileen was only eighteen, he was twenty-three. He was sure of his feelings, but she wasn't. She'd led a fairly sheltered life and this was her first real friendship with a man. Not only that, Cedric's college discouraged ordinands from getting engaged or marrying while still in training.

"I can't tell you everything, I don't want to be disloyal to my brother. All I can say is that the friendship ended and Cedric came to the conclusion the college was right. From that moment on he declared himself a confirmed bachelor and swore he'd remain celibate for the rest of his life."

We were interrupted by one of the doctors. It was good news. The pain was under control, Cedric was asleep, and they'd be operating the following morning. There was nothing more we could do and the doctor suggested we come back the next day. Before leaving we looked in on Cedric and, sure enough, he was sleeping peacefully.

Back in Ashenridge, Mrs Batchelor was having a very busy time of it. Still unaware that the venue had been changed, she borrowed the parish hall key and waited there for the van to deliver the choicest of flowers and greenery she'd ordered the previous day. Oh how she relished the thought of decorating the hall for the meeting with the bishop. What a lovely surprise for everyone. This would certainly be an evening to remember.

Steven dropped me back at the rectory and I got there only minutes before the bishop arrived. Later, as I drove him to Brookworthy, I told him about Cedric. He didn't seem that surprised.

"I believe your curate has been unwell in more ways than one of late. I did suggest he see a doctor, but these young men are all the same. I sincerely hope things go well for him now. Do give him my good wishes."

Not one member of the six Church Councils had been put off at the thought of sitting on the uncomfortable seats at Brookworthy Parish Hall. Every one of them had turned up, except poor Mrs Batchelor who learned too late about the change of venue.

The council members were alarmed to hear that Cedric was in hospital. Many of us had been worrying about him for weeks, and a grumbling appendix went a long way towards explaining his recent odd behaviour. Before the meeting the bishop asked that we pray together for Cedric, for a successful operation and a quick and full recovery.

The Badger Group was the first of its kind in the diocese and it was rewarding to hear the bishop's words of praise.

However, before setting up any similar groupings he was keen to hear from the members how things were progressing.

There was a strained silence, the opportunity to speak having come sooner than expected. I could see several people bracing themselves and one or two pulled out scraps of paper with carefully prepared notes on them.

One man complained about the iniquities of the parishes being expected to pay for the repairs to the rectory drive.

Another held forth about services starting late.

This was followed by another council member stating it was shameful her Aunt Polly had spent several days in Whiteminster Hospital with a broken toe and neither of the clergy had taken the trouble to visit her.

This was all pretty predictable stuff, but the bishop listened carefully, occasionally correcting a statement or promising action if he thought it necessary.

Then Miss Pringle was invited to speak. This was the bit I'd been dreading. She rose to her feet and looked around the hall, her spectacles, as always, perched on the end of her nose.

"I speak not as a parishioner, but as a member of the Bishop's Council who happens to live in Ashenridge."

I was taken aback. I had no idea she was a member of that august body.

"When I moved to this parish I expected a visit from one of the clergy within the first week. I expected to find the church in spotless order, displaying the correct altar frontal, offering a service at the right time and to my taste. I was told by some this did not happen because the rector was a lazy, money-grabbing empire builder.

"I was also told that although he had the help of a curate, the parishioners and churches were grossly neglected. I visited the rectory with its badly potholed drive and was told he had the temerity to expect the locals to donate money to repair it."

At the mention of the drive people started muttering amongst themselves. This promised to be a much more interesting meeting than the members had ever imagined. We might even get to the truth.

"At this juncture I happened to meet a churchwarden from one of the other parishes. He told me their parish bitterly resented being dictated to by a distant rector. They had a perfectly good priest of their own living in Westaleigh who should be left alone to carry on with his work.

"Word soon got round that I was known to you, my Lord Bishop, and that I was also highly critical of what was going on in these churches. Consequently, in my short time here I have been approached by some who feel they have reasonable grounds for complaint against the rector and his curate. One or two complained that Mr Longfield was running the village shop when he should have been taking a funeral, that he is frequently late for services, and that he quite happily goes off for a day's outing with his family when everybody else is working. I am given to understand that he likes to take it easy on a Sunday and that is the reason he sometimes has only one service for the whole group. A minority believe that by doing this he is stealthily paving the way to close half of his churches and still be paid the same."

Miss Pringle paused. Some people smiled, some looked awkward, others looked angry. I guessed she had not finished.

"My Lord Bishop, I must confess I was mistaken. I moved to this lovely area knowing very little about country churches. I assumed that life here was easy for the clergy. The grass seemed to grow so much greener for them than their urban counterparts. In my ignorance I sympathised with those who made complaints. Then I realised my mistake. In this gathering there are representatives from not one but six different churches. Not that long ago five full-time clergy served them, but now the church can no longer afford to employ so many. Yet the two remaining priests are expected to carry on as before.

"Since Ashenridge Hall is booked almost every day, it's not surprising that we are forced to sit on these uncomfortable benches in the only available hall.   I suppose we could have met in a church, but those ancient buildings are hardly suitable for ordinary meetings, especially as they are very expensive to heat in the winter. The consequence is that our rector has made his home available for all kinds of gatherings. I hear there are occasions when as many as three events can be going on at the rectory simultaneously.   I would therefore ask the diocese to think twice before replacing it, and the parishes to be a little more understanding over the cost of repairing potholes.

"I have one or two things to say that relate particularly to Westaleigh. I understand that this parish would like to break away from the Badger Group. Apart from the need to raise a sum quite beyond them to pay for their own rector and maintain his house, I would like them to consider what they would lose. I'll select just one thing, something that must be unique in today's rural parishes. I am, of course, referring to the Holiday Club.   It couldn't happen without all the parishes pulling together. You are the envy of many other rural parishes. I appeal to you, do not destroy what is good."

Miss Pringle sat down to a round of applause even she hadn't expected, and the bishop stood to give his considered response.

"A man in his first curacy is very much a learner, an apprentice. It probably is a mistake for a beginner like Mr Palmer to move into a vicarage miles away from other clergy. Inevitably, the parishioners expect him to act as a vicar in his own right, and he himself will be tempted to take on that role. I want to stress that you have been most fortunate in the very loyal behaviour of the two curates I sent you."

This would be good news to take back to Cedric. Sir William Radlett was looking slightly awkward. He was afraid they would now lose Westaleigh Vicarage altogether, and it would be his fault for making such a fuss. He looked relieved as the bishop continued.

"I had once planned to dispose of the excellent vicarage at Westaleigh, but then I had second thoughts. The Badger Group is growing, may even get bigger. If so it will need more clergy, and they cannot all be beginners. I therefore plan that when Mr Palmer leaves us the vicarage should be reserved for a more experienced priest who will work alongside Jack Longfield and any future curate.

"This brings me to the question of the rectory. Normally parishes that have curates are expected to pay for the accommodation. So far I have exempted the parishes here from doing that. I believe that any future curate should live in Ashenridge – the same parish as the rector. And the solution seems obvious. Either create a flat at the rear of the rectory or build a separate property in the grounds. This will inevitably involve greater use of the drive and I therefore have no hesitation in recommending that the diocese should pay the full costs of having it repaired."

As with Miss Pringle, the bishop's words were met with a round of applause. I was not sure whether the bishop and Miss Pringle had simple taken the wind out of everyone's sails, or whether it was the uncomfortable wooden benches, but nobody wanted to prolong the meeting and it finished well before nine.

Unlike the meeting in Ashenridge Parish Hall which went on until well after nine-thirty. When the ladies turned up they simply could not believe their eyes. Floral displays cascaded from every windowsill, and pots and vases bursting with blooms had been dotted around the rest of the hall.

Mrs Batchelor appeared wearing one of her Ascot hats. She warmly greeted the astonished ladies, assuming they were there to provide cups of tea for the meeting with the bishop. It took the WI members some time convincing her that the venue had been changed to Brookworthy.

The ladies rose to the occasion and Mrs Batchelor was made an honorary member of the Women's Institute. In the absence of a speaker she entertained them for the next two hours, happily talking about the joys of flower arranging and floral decorations, and it was gone nine-thirty before the improvised meeting – or as Len Cooksley had put it 'impoverished' meeting – came to an end.

Steven rang me early the next day with good news. Cedric's operation had gone well and he was making a full recovery. I visited that evening and Cedric looked a different man. The colour had returned to his cheeks, as had his familiar smile.

He began by apologising again, saying there was no excuse for his bad behaviour.

"Perhaps I should be the one to apologise. I'd no idea you'd been feeling so unwell until Miss Pringle told me everything. Perhaps we've both been at fault. One thing though, if you have any more problems, don't forget where I am."

We chatted happily and I updated Cedric on the events of the previous evening – how we'd all joined together in prayers for him, the fine reception the bishop and Miss Pringle had received. I promised to visit again in a couple of days, and left him chuckling over the outcome of Mrs Batchelor's latest surprise.

My next visit didn't go quite as planned. Cedric looked well enough, but his eyes kept glazing over and he had a permanent grin on his face. I could have been forgiven for thinking some of the anaesthetic was still in his system.

We sat in silence for a few minutes and I wondered if it might be better to come back another day. The nurse taking Cedric's pulse had been holding on to his wrist for much longer than was necessary and, what's more, I now realised she wore the same glazed look and the same silly grin.

I couldn't wait to get home and tell Mary the good news. Cedric Palmer, the confirmed bachelor, had fallen in love with the prettiest nurse in Whiteminster General Hospital, and I could see from the look on her face the feeling was completely mutual.

Chapter 20

Dinner for Two

Little did Kitty know the surprise that was in store for her on the day of Ashenridge Flower Show. The show was one of the highlights of her year, and she and her friends from the bus shelter were happy to help with whatever jobs were allocated to them.

This year saw a record number of entries and everyone was praying for good weather. As always, the committee had been hard at work and Mary was given the task of finding prizes for the draw. People had been more than generous knowing that this year's proceeds would be going to the Ashenridge Church Fund.

The day was hot and sunny and at two o'clock on the dot Colonel Waters opened the show. People went dashing off in all directions, and those who had entered the various classes made a beeline for the marquee to see how they'd fared in the judging. If only there had been an appropriate class, Mrs Batchelor's stunning straw hat would easily have taken first prize. She'd decorated it with bunches of scarlet cherries, sprigs of purple lilac and tiny white daisies. How did she keep it looking so fresh in the afternoon sun?

The catering team did a roaring trade in ice creams and fizzy drinks. The demand for cream teas was so great the ladies nearly ran out of strawberry jam. Children and adults alike enjoyed the games, and our dear friends, Henry and Stephanie

Burrows, came over from Leighford to lend a hand. I'd never seen Ashenridge Flower Show so busy.

The grand draw was due to take place at five and the show secretary asked if I would call out the winning numbers. What a display. Bottles of sherry, whisky and wine, baskets of fruit, potted plants, tins of biscuits, and two magnificent hampers which had been donated by Mr & Mrs Radd – their way of saying thank you for all the help they'd received at the village shop during Mrs Radd's illness. Mary had done a great job – no wonder so many tickets had been sold.

I stood on an upturned box clutching a plastic bucket. "Ladies and gentlemen, before I start the draw I want to say a big thank you to the committee for a splendid afternoon. I can't remember a better flower show. We've certainly been blessed with superb weather. Thanks must go to all the committee members and their helpers, and to all of you for supporting the show."

Without further ado I plucked the first ticket from the bucket. "The top prize goes to blue ticket number 44."

Mary and a few others who were busy clearing the tea tables stopped what they were doing to look at their tickets. Mary nudged Kitty excitedly. "That's you. You've won first prize."

Kitty went charging out of the tea-tent, her right arm propelling her along, and collected the first prize to a huge round of applause. For an awful moment I thought she was going to ask if she could swap the pink envelope for one of the hampers, but she obviously thought better of it.

Knowing what was inside the envelope, Mary caught hold of her. "Go on then Kitty, open it."

Kitty wasn't that good a reader and she passed the contents of the envelope to Mary. "How wonderful. It says you've won a dinner for two at The Grand Palace Hotel in Whiteminster."

Kitty wasn't too sure about this. Maybe she should have asked to exchange it for a hamper after all, then seeing the collection of pink, blue and yellow raffle tickets in Mary's hand exclaimed, "Cor, makes yer think don' it. 'Ere's me winning first prize with only one ticket an' you got nothin'. Don't seem fair, do it?"

"What you goin' to wear, Kitty? You can't wear that old cardigan."

Kitty shuffled. "Tell yer the truth, I'm a bit short on dresses right now."

"What about your teeth? You says you 'as some, but us's never seen 'em."

"Who're you takin' with you, Len Cooksley?" This suggestion brought gales of laughter.

"And 'ow about a four-course dinner. Reck'n it'll make you sick."

Nobody was going to make a fool out of Kitty. She'd never had much luck, and come what may she was going to make the most of her prize. But she did have one or two problems to sort out, like what to wear and who to take with her.

Annie Cook resolved the first problem and found something for Kitty to wear. A blue silk dress with a matching handbag, the likes of which Kitty had only ever seen in magazines. Now all she had to do was find a partner. Her first choice was Len Cooksley, but he refused on the grounds he didn't have a car.

"Reck'n I 'ad a narrow escape there, rector," he chortled at me a few days later. "I likes Kitty enough, but they posh places ain't for me with their hairy fairy ways."

Perhaps Mr Radd could take her in his delivery van, but on second thoughts Mrs Radd might object. Rumour had it I was next on the list.

"He's here again," Mary hissed at me through gritted teeth. Mary was none too happy that cousin Will had made another surprise visit. "Last time he nearly had us out of our home. We're lucky we didn't lose the rectory. It's no good, Jack, you'll have to deal with him."

I could understand Mary's concern. It had been a close shave when Will inadvertently led Peter Eastridge to believe I was either about to leave the parish or be promoted to the rank of bishop. The powers that be didn't need much of an excuse to get us out of our home, especially as they believed the rectory drive was going to cost them a fortune to repair. Mary was right, Will had almost brought the Longfield family to a sticky end, but despite his failings I knew he meant no harm.

I could see from the look on his face Will was feeling low. "I don't know why Mary's so worried. I haven't come to stay. I'm delivering a car in Whiteminster and thought I'd stop by to say hello." Through the drawing-room window I could see a brand new Bentley parked in the drive.

"You know I didn't get that job Sir William put me up for. I suppose it went to a better man. Times are pretty bad, Jack. This is the way I earn a crust these days. Matter of fact I'll be back again in November delivering another car. Suppose I'd be pushing my luck if I asked for a bed for the night?"

"You most certainly would not."

I was prepared to risk the backlash from Mary because a brilliant idea had come to me.

"You'll be more than welcome, but in return I'm going to ask you to do me a favour. How do you fancy a four-course dinner at The Grand Palace Hotel in Whiteminster?"

"By Jove, you sky pilots must be doing well." Will was back to his old self and started laughing. "Have they finally discovered your real worth and given you a pay rise?"

"Well it's not quite like that. You see, we have a queen living here in our village and she's looking for a prince to escort her to dinner."

"Going to tell me who she is? Not trying to marry me off are you?"

I described Kitty in the only way I knew and I could see Will was intrigued.

On a cold winter's evening Will called for Kitty. She didn't notice the neighbours' curtains twitching as she left the house; she hardly remembered Becky giving her a hug as she said goodbye. But she did remember the journey in a brand new Bentley as it purred its way to The Grand Palace Hotel in Whiteminster. When they arrived she was still clutching the box of Cadbury's chocolates Will had given her.

"What should I call yer then?"

"Well, most people call me Will. Some call me William. The Longfield children call me Uncle Tiddly, though I can't for the life of me think why."

"Well, I can't call yer Uncle Tiddly 'cause yer not me uncle. I'll call yer William."

Kitty had never set foot in such a magnificent place. The Grand Palace Hotel really was like a palace. Naturally she felt a little nervous, but Will quickly put her at ease – and the two schooners of Harveys Bristol Cream probably helped. She chuckled to herself as she thought of the pint of stout she normally drank at home of an evening. Not that long ago she enjoyed a cigarette with a drink, but her granddaughter, Becky, had put paid to that with her dreadful nagging. All the same she was gasping for one right now.

Kitty's worst moment came when they entered the restaurant and she was confronted with a bewildering array of cutlery and glasses. She nudged Will and pointed to her limp arm. Noticing her anxiety Will said, "Don't you worry, Kitty. Everything's been taken care of."

Kitty didn't fancy a prawn cocktail or grapefruit for starters.

"What about the consommé." suggested Will helpfully.

"Consommé?" What the 'ell's that?"

"It's a sort of soup."

Kitty liked soup, but when it arrived it looked more like cabbage water – didn't taste bad though.

For the fish course, instead of a hearty chunk of battered cod a small helping of whitebait appeared on her plate. "What about the chips and vinegar?" she asked none too quietly, looking for the waiter. She stared at the tiny fish and they stared back at her. Was she supposed to eat them, eyes and all?

At that moment her own eyes nearly popped out of her head as she recognised the young couple sitting on the other side of the room. Will followed her gaze.

"Tell yer who 'e is. 'E's Cedric Palmer, young parson from Westaleigh. 'E don' know me, but I sees 'im round. Cor, fancy comin' 'ere for 'is dinner."

"You're right, he's Jack's curate. But who's the lady with him?"

"'Tis that nurse from the general 'ospital who looked after 'im when 'is appendix came out. She was with 'im at the flower show."

All this was too good to be true – even better than sitting in the bus shelter gossiping with her friends. "I could tell yer a thing or two 'bout 'e. Made a right scummer when 'e got hisself drunk."

Kitty was finding it hard to sit still and forgetting herself grabbed a handful of whitebait and shoved them in her mouth.

By the time the main course arrived Kitty was in a fine state. Her eyes were glued to Cedric Palmer and his lady friend. But even they couldn't stop her enjoying the plateful of roast beef, especially as someone had been kind enough to cut it up so nicely for her. Will nearly choked when Kitty calmly removed her teeth and put them back in their dirty old box.

What with the sherry before dinner, the wine during dinner and now the sherry in the trifle, it was all getting a bit too much. Kitty kicked Will under the table. "Look, 'e's got a box too. Probably got false teeth like mine. Wait for it, I reck'n 'e's goin' to take 'em out."

"No, take another look," whispered an excited Will, who, like Kitty, couldn't take his eyes off the couple. "That box is far too small for a set of teeth. Can't you see what he's putting on her finger?"

Kitty could see only too well, and what she saw brought her close to tears. She looked down at her limp hand and the dainty ring that hadn't left her finger in over fifty years. She pictured a time long ago when she and Charlie went for a picnic on Ashenridge Moor. Charlie had sat her down on an old tree trunk, fumbled for the ring in his trouser pocket and said: "Got a ring 'ere, Kitty. Thought us'd get married. What do yer think girl?"

She'd leapt off that tree trunk and kissed Charlie 'til he could hardly breathe. Poor Charlie, why did he have to suffer and be taken from her like that with typhoid, and them married less than three years?

Will's voice brought her back to the present. "My word, Kitty. Look, she's accepted. Cedric's slipping the ring on her finger."

Cedric Palmer and Nurse Patricia wouldn't have noticed if a herd of elephants had charged through the restaurant. The newly-engaged couple were too busy sipping Champagne and gazing into each other's eyes.

Kitty brushed the tears from her eyes with the linen napkin then blew her nose loudly into it. What a b...y shame tomorrow was Sunday. She'd have to wait a whole day before sharing this bit of juicy gossip with her friends in the bus shelter.

She gave a deep sigh. "Reck'n us'll soon be 'earin' weddin' bells for they two." Kitty sighed again. "Thank yer, William, I've 'ad a smashin' evenin'. Can't remember when I enjoyed meself so much. An' dunno 'bout you, but I loves a story with an 'appy endin'."

COMING 2009
THE GREEN GRASS OF SUMMER
Christopher Tull

Set between 1966 and 1973, *The Green Grass of Summer* is the continuing story of Jack Longfield's ministry at Ashenridge Church and five other parishes in the West Country.

With the departure of his curate, Jack is finding life pretty difficult. Unfortunately, the new Bishop of Whiteminster is in no hurry to take on another curate, but following his visit to Ashenridge Church on Easter Sunday he has a change of heart and Tim Ashman is appointed as team vicar. Tim likes all things modern and thinks he has the answer to everything, until he meets the new headmaster of Ashenridge Primary School, who bears an uncanny resemblance to Fidel Castro.

When a problem curate by the name of Harry Browne is appointed, Jack immediately takes him under his wing. Untidy, disorganised, unreliable, Harry is on the point of being sacked for missing his own welcoming service. But there's more to Harry than meets the eye.

Peter Eastridge and Sir William Radlett continue their anti-Longfield campaign. Uncle Tiddly passes out on Mrs Batchelor's drawing-room floor having drunk a whole bottle of Harveys Bristol Cream. And then there's the cheeky baker's boy who calls every girl sweetheart, until one takes him too seriously. These are some of Jack's finest years in Ashenridge. But the Longfield family know only too well that life in a rural parish isn't always a bed of roses...